NORTHERN BEACHES WRITERS' GROUP

The Northern Beaches Writers' Group is an award-winning writing critique group based in Sydney. We're online at:

northernbeacheswritersgroup.com
facebook.com/northernbeacheswritersgroup

VILLAIN

OR

HERO?

STORIES TO
MAKE YOU
WONDER WHICH...

EDITED BY

ZENA SHAPTER

Villain or Hero?

First published in Australia 2023 by
the Northern Beaches Writers' Group, Sydney.

Cover design & internal design by Zena Shapter.

The characters in this book are fictitious and any resemblance to real
persons, living or dead, is purely coincidental.

CONTENTS

BECAUSE LABELS DO NOT
DEFINE WHO WE ARE...

FOREWORD

ZENA SHAPTER

In our storytelling past, a typical villain was a one-dimensional character offering readers little more than evil demeanours, wicked thoughts and nefarious plans. They might have suffered deeply damaging trauma in their past, but this was rarely explored beyond how much it consumed them and disabled them from recognising the reprehensible nature of their despicable behaviours. They took their pain and hurt the world with it.

No more! One of the greatest joys in contemporary storytelling is delving deeper into the lives of archetypal villains, exploring what makes them who they are, and deepening their experience within the conversation of story. We all feel pain and experience trauma. We all have failings and make mistakes. We all suffer. We also all love and hope. Examining the nature of villainy is thus a method of examining the nature of what it means to be human.

Perhaps the only real difference between hero and villain is timing, or perspective, or who gets to recount certain events. Our own actions and words are often widely interpreted by others, regardless of our intentions.

Thus the thirteen stories in these pages set out to challenge traditional villain archetypes with transformative retellings, backstories or alternate viewpoints, expressed as entirely original creative works.

One person's villain can be another's hero!

Let's probe the pasts, thoughts, and alternate worlds of character types we're supposed to hate. Let's explore what made them who they are or want to be. Let's imagine what they would say if asked, what they would do if observed anew. Let's take these tales of fantasy, romance, crime, thriller, science fiction, historical fiction, and go on a storytelling adventure...

Zena Shapter
Editor-in-Chief

BURNING BRIGHT

cb

AISLINN MCKENZIE

Bagh felt unsettled. He raised his head from the river, water dripping down his white chin as he breathed in the smell of the mangroves. His ears twitched as he listened to the unnaturally quiet surrounds. Over the past few weeks, there had been an oppressive denseness to the air that felt like a thick fog hanging over the jungle. Something new had come. Bagh had seen it in one of the nearby villages. It looked much like the other manfolk, but with skin like the flesh of pale fish.

Bagh lowered his head and waded into the river, grateful for the cool mud and water, which soothed his singed paws and face. He had come from the meeting at Council Rock, where the foolish man cub Mowgli had carelessly brandished a branch of the Red Flower. But it was of no concern now. The Council had decided that Mowgli was a man, and he must return to the village to live with his own kind. Bagh chuffed heartily to himself as he swam forwards into the middle of the river. Mowgli had been a thorn in his side for ten seasons, and his return to the village meant less humans interfering in the jungle.

Dusk was beginning to fall as Bagh reached the deepest section of the river, eddies twirling around him with each powerful stroke. In the water, no animal could call him that cruel epithet, *Lungri*, the Lame One; he moved as if weightless. As darkness fell, spheres of blue light rose out of the water and disappeared between the reeds and limbs of the mangroves to wander the jungle. These were the Aleya lights, the spirits of drowned fishermen now serving as the watchful eyes of Dakshin Rai, Lord of the South and ruler of the Land of Eighteen Tides. Bagh submerged his head into the rippling light and, when he resurfaced, the burns on his face had vanished and his eyes shone like the silver scales of a fish. Some of the Aleya lights hovered around Bagh, tickling his ears and resting on his back. He shook his head to shoo them away but they returned, persistent, and his feelings of misgiving returned. An Aleya light flittered ahead of him and waited on a branch, leaping up as he drew closer. Breathing a long sigh, Bagh slowly followed the spirit deep into the heart of the jungle.

In this part of the jungle, the mangroves grew large and twisted, encasing the river within a wooden ribcage. Not even moonlight could penetrate the tangled canopy. Bagh felt as if he were swimming through the blackness between stars. When the Aleya spirits began to pulse with fervent energy, Bagh hoped it signalled the end of their journey. He dared not stray too far into the heart of the jungle, for great gods and creatures still crept along the riverbeds and slept under the perfumed bushes. Most of all he feared Bonbibi, the Lady of the Forest, and Dakshin Rai's greatest adversary. It was she who had long ago crushed his paw to limit the powers granted him by Dakshin Rai.

The banks of the river grew narrower until Bagh felt the mangrove limbs brushing up against his side. Ahead of him the Aleya had finally stopped inside a cavernous chamber made from the roots of an ancient tree. As Bagh slunk inside the chamber, the water began to smell and cling to his fur. Heart pounding, he raised his lip, flashing his teeth and snarling at the putrid darkness. The riverbed rose to meet his paws as he limped up the bank. Streams of reeking blood formed a delta in the dark sand and he moved cautiously around it. Ahead, the soft light of the Aleya cast a pallid glow upon a grey mass. Even with his great eyes, it took Bagh some moments before he realised what was before him. Slippery and pink, no heads nor tails. Bagh nudged it with his nose and the mass broke apart, the bodies of skinned tigers slipping towards him. Bagh roared in terror, leaping back into the water. The Aleya lights whirled above him, then plunged inside the maw of a tiger which still had its head.

Bones creaked beneath its taut skin as it slowly pulled itself up to a tremendous height, towering over Bagh. The blue light shone from its empty eye sockets and hanging broken jaw.

"O Raja Bagh, descendant of Dakshin Rai, his soul upon this plane, look what they have done to us," called the tiger spirit. Its voice echoed around him, filling him with maddening horror. The dead tiger moved haphazardly towards him, its limp body struggling to balance. It brought its face close to his and touched his cheek while making soothing chuffing noises. "Do not be frightened, I beg you," said the spirit.

Bagh hesitantly returned the gesture, his cheek becoming wet with the tiger's blood. As he touched its face, his fear ebbed away, replaced by a tremendous grief. "Did a king do this to you?" he asked, for he knew of the manfolk tradition that bid their rulers kill a tiger to prove their strength.

"It is the four newcomers," the spirit replied. "They do not respect the balance between manfolk and the jungle. Even Bonbibi, protector of the fishermen, is sickened by them and wants them gone from our lands."

"Where are they now?"

"They have made settlement in the manfolk village north of the River Halda. You will know them by their pale heads and red coats."

"Then I will go and kill them," replied Bagh.

But the spirit shook its head, its bones cracking like dry, autumn twigs. "Do not be so rash. You must be wary of the man cub, for he too resides in that village. He has already learned the trickery of humans," sighed the spirit, its voice weakening. "We tigers are proud, powerful animals, please do not let us die so dishonourably."

The Aleya light faded and the tiger's body fell motionless onto the riverbank.

Bagh stood for a moment in the darkness before turning from the chamber and swimming back down the river.

Dawn was breaking when Bagh pulled himself back out of the water. He lay motionless on the silty bank, his head hot and his limbs beyond fatigued. A few remaining Aleya lights rested on his body, avoiding the flick of his tail. The Aleya pulsed brighter with each pound of his heart until Bagh could see nothing of his surroundings and his head was filled with heavy light. The snarls of Dakshin Rai grumbled deep within him and this time not even Bonbibi could silence him. Bagh's insides burned with fire as he rose, drawing himself to his full height and roaring into the morning, shaking the earth. The whole jungle fell silent and Bagh sensed that even the Gecho Bhoot, the ghosts of the trees, were watching him now. It had been a long time since such a powerful spirit had made itself known and the dying rumble of Bagh's roar awoke them from their slumber. Bagh shook off the remaining Aleya and made his way to the manfolk village.

It took several hours to reach the craggy path up to the village, but Bagh did not tire. The village sat atop a plateau with deep ravines on either side. The newcomers had built their bungalow along a ridge next to a paddock filled with buffalo. Bagh snuffed impatiently, picking his way through the tree line to stay upwind of the tamed beasts. He caught Mowgli's scent on the wind, sweaty and dog-like. He thought he could also detect the stink of a wolf, but he convinced himself it was simply the man cub. He snuffed, clearing the smell from his nostrils.

He climbed between the large branches of an old jackfruit tree and lay across it, staying hidden while he watched the pallid manfolk. The four of them frequented a large enclosed vat, within which the other men of the village churned blue water. Those in the water looked devoid of flesh, their bones barely held together by their skin. Bagh could hear an argument between a newcomer and a villager who had pulled himself from the vat. The newcomer took out a long sword and was holding it up to the villager. Suddenly there was a flash of metal and Bagh flattened his ears as the villager screamed. The man collapsed to the ground, his dismembered hand now a limp claw on the earth beside him. Bagh looked down at his own lame paw. He could not afford to be complacent around these newcomers or their weapons.

Night brought with it a heavy mist and the choiring of cicadas and frogs. Two of the newcomers had taken up watch at the front of the bungalow, while the other two retreated inside.

His stomach churning with the fire of Dakshin Rai, Bagh exhaled a puff of smoke through his nostrils as he jumped down onto the pathway and slunk towards the bungalow. The veranda creaked under his weight, but the red-coated men remained oblivious, chattering to each other like monkeys. Bagh crept towards an open window, his eyes flashing silver under the lamplight. Inside, the manfolk lounged with their red coats open and cheeks ruddy from drink, guffawing amid a haze of acrid pipe smoke. Underneath the smell of smoke lingered the scent of a dozen striped pelts, stretched across their walls.

Bagh pounced through the window, smoke billowing from his mouth as he roared. The manfolk toppled off their chairs, yelping in terror, and Bagh advanced on them, the fire deep within him reflected in their wide eyes. The manfolk nearest him broke first, trying to crawl away, but Bagh slashed deep into the man's thigh, hooking his claws into him to drag him back before biting into his neck. He wrenched the head clean from the human's torso and looked up at the other manfolk, blood dripping from his mouth.

The other one lunged at him with a shaking sword, managing to slice across Bagh's face. Bagh bellowed and stumbled, pawing at his cheek while the manfolk hooted in triumph. Blue lights slipped through the windows, collecting on Bagh's bleeding face, knitting his wound, and the manfolk's smile faltered. He raised his sword again, but Bagh batted it from his grip and closed his jaws on his chest, splintering his ribs.

There was a loud crash behind him, and he whirled around as the remaining two newcomers ran inside, brandishing their metal sticks. The night air ripped with two deafening cracks, and Bagh felt something hot bite into his legs, causing him to collapse. The manfolk inched towards him with raised knives, mistaking him finished. As they drew close, Bagh lunged towards them, crushing one against a table and breaking open his face, before locking his jaws around the skull of the other. With the last of his strength, the man twisted his arm up and buried his knife into Bagh's eye. The blade clattered to the floor, it's owner finally still.

A cacophony of pain drummed within Bagh's head, white splotches of light flashing across his broken vision, muddled with the blue Aleya. They hummed and moved around him, trying to heal his wound, but the cut was too great. He lifted his head and looked out the window as the veranda creaked outside.

Streaked with dirt and grime, a look of resolution upon his face, was Mowgli. Clasped in his hand was a branch of the Red Flower, which he tossed into the bungalow.

Almost immediately the wooden floors and walls caught alight. Bagh yowled as the flames grew before him. He staggered to his paws and dragged himself towards the door, pushing against it with all his might as the heat curled his fur into a matted mess. The door buckled under his weight and he crashed onto the veranda before pulling himself away from the flaming building.

Mowgli stood before him surrounded by his wolf pack, Bagheera and Baloo.

Bagh sprawled before them, his breathing shallow and laboured, and his white chest soaked red with blood.

"You have done enough, Shere Khan," Mowgli yelled. "It is time for you to die."

The animals of the jungle all readied themselves to fight at Mowgli's words.

Bagh glared at each of them in turn.

"You listen to this brat?" he roared. "You are all fools! Mowgli is human. He does not belong in our jungle. Are we not allowed a space for ourselves? To hunt and be wild animals? These humans ruin our lands with their industry, turn our sweet water blue with indigo."

As Bagh spoke, Akela, leader of the wolves, slunk away into

the trees with a nasty glint in his eyes. No matter. That wolf was the reason Mowgli still lived in their jungle, Aklea would not be persuaded by him.

"They tear out our teeth," Bagh shouted after him, "and break our claws, wrench our skin from our flesh, simply for following our traditions. Mowgli has softened you and now you do nothing to protect our jungle."

"You know the jungle law," called Bagheera. "We do not attack the manfolk, for then the villagers hunt us and the white men will bring their guns. Everybody in the jungle suffers."

"Do you all believe the insipid tales of Mowgli? We have only ever hunted to feed ourselves. These newcomers kill us as if it were a game!" roared Bagh. "Our actions should not be at fault. It is manfolk's unending hatred for a world they cannot control. It is their insatiable hearts. Who taught you these jungle laws? Who were the ones that killed us if we didn't follow?"

This time no protest followed his words. The animals were unsettled by his words, for they could not remember the way the jungle had been before the manfolk arrived.

"Enough, Shere Khan," Mowgli shouted, advancing.

"I will not be tamed," Bagh roared, his fur bristling, his shadow lengthening under the moonlight. He rose before them, showing the creatures of the jungle his true self. The tiger before them was not Shere Khan the cowardly tiger, but Bagh the spirit of Dakshin Rai.

They whimpered and bowed their heads in disgrace, filled with self-loathing and confusion.

Mowgli looked at the animals around him with surprise and contempt. "Why do you debase yourself for this coward?"

"Hush Mowgli," hissed Bagheera. "You don't understand the old lore of the jungle."

Mowgli's face reddened and he cast his eyes down.

"There is still time to change this, Mowgli," sighed Bagh, his breathing laboured.

Mowgli looked up, his face contorted with indecision. He made to speak but his words were drowned out by a yapping and snarling from behind them. Akela had stalked behind the buffalo in the neighbouring paddock, and now nipped at their heels, causing them to bellow in terror. They snapped their heads around, trying to track the wolf with bulging white eyes. They stumbled, picking up speed, unable to go anywhere but towards the bungalow.

Mowgli leapt astride Bagheera, and he and the other animals vanished into the surrounding trees. Broken and bloodied, Bagh raised his head to the oncoming stampede and waited.

Eventually, the dust settled and a quiet hung over the village, more pronounced after the cacophony of raging animals. It as a silence that Mowgli had never heard before, plangent and unsettling. All the manfolk emerged cautiously from their homes to inspect the carnage of the bungalow. Upon seeing the corpses of the British, relief appeared on their faces and they all started talking in hushed excitement.

Mowgli pushed his way through the villagers to the matted

dusty heap of fur, barely recognisable as the once proud Shere Khan. He knelt beside the broken tiger and brandished the knife he kept in a pouch around his waist. A group of villagers had curiously followed him and, as he pulled the knife out of its sheath, an elder of the village rushed forward.

"O Babu, my son, please leave this animal. It has helped us in ways you don't understand," he said, placing a knobbly hand on Mowgli's shoulder.

Mowgli snarled at him and flicked his hand away. "I killed him, I have every right," he said and, grabbing a fistful of the tiger's fur beneath its chin, he proceeded to slice the animal down to its crumpled belly. As the knife sliced through Bagh's flesh, a wave of nausea and vertigo temporarily overcame Mowgli. He dropped the knife, his heart pounding in his ears. He shook his head and continued. With shaking hands, Mowgli lifted the pelt, only to scramble back as large burning embers tumbled onto the ground, before deadening to charred bones.

The elder gave a soft cry and the villagers gasped in horror. Mowgli lifted the pelt and peered inside the beast. It was hollow, as if the creature had been powered by fire.

The old man behind him whispered a prayer. "This is a terrible deed," he croaked, tears welling in his aged eyes. "You have desecrated the spirit of Dakshin Rai. These are our spirits, Babu, they protect these lands and maintain the balance between humans and nature. You and the jungle creatures have lost your way. The soldiers have blinded your hearts, so that you bend beneath their laws. Although this tiger has removed some of our pain, I fear that we all have a longer journey ahead of us now. You have acted rashly and these actions will have grave consequences."

Mowgli looked to Akela and the wolves for guidance, but they stood there with their heads lowered and their tails tucked between their legs.

"What does this mean, Akela?" Mowgli asked, fear now creeping inside his heart.

Akela tilted his head and tried to reply but Mowgli could not understand. All he heard was the whimpering noise of an animal. Tears welled in Mowgli's eyes as he stumbled backwards, searching the faces of the jungle creatures and villagers. But no answers could be found there, only unease and silence.

Mowgli aggressively brushed his tears away and lifted his chin. He rose shakily to his feet and looked briefly to his wolfpack before disappearing into the shadows of the jungle.

ABOUT 'BURNING BRIGHT'

This story was inspired by my partner Monjer, who grew up in Bangladesh and came to Australia by himself at eighteen. His knowledge of Bangladeshi folklore and mythology have influenced my characterisation of Bagh and the ethereal mangrove landscape. I've incorporated elements of his childhood, such as the Halda river he grew up near, as well as his family's stories and experiences of living under the British Raj. Monjer often speaks of the lasting impacts that colonisation has had upon people's self-worth in the subcontinent and I wanted explored this through Mowgli and the jungle animals. After all of the great stories he has told me, I felt it was time I wrote one for him.

ABOUT AISLINN McKENZIE

Aislinn McKenzie is a reclusive Sydney-based human who recounts all of her former peculiar unwanted encounters with warlocks, talking toads and cursed deities. It appears however, that these accounts have been interpreted as fiction by the general populace and as a result she has had some success with her writing. Her short story 'The Old Dog' was published in the Macquarie University Journal *The Quarry*, while her short story 'The Dusty Veteran' was publish in the magazine *The Village Observer*. Her other works have been in the top 5 for the *New York Midnight Writers* challenge. She will continue to write until a kind witch stumbles upon her work and can help her create a spell to keep these strange happenings from disturbing her peace.

STONE HEARTED

———⌇———

A.R KELLY

"Do you have it?" Cybilla asked in her saccharine voice, stretching her lacquered claws out towards me.

I swallowed the urge to flinch as she placed her wrinkly gnarled fingers on my wrist with the familiarity of an old friend. But she was not my friend. On my lap, under the table, my other hand held tight to the knuckle-sized gold coin that I had worked so hard to liberate. This one had been a challenge to find, and a lot of blood had been turned into stone in separating this treasure from its last owner.

I pushed back into the plush velvet sofa, and watched as she smiled and preened at the young men and women who caught her eye as they wandered past our table. The clinking of glass and gentle chatter insulated us from the eternal chaos of the city outside. A city that felt less like home each time I returned to it.

The air surrounding Cybilla seemed to waver and shimmer like the haze over the ocean on a hot summer's day. Despite all the work she had done to change her appearance over the years, the menacing air of a predator hung thick over her no matter how innocent she looked physically, the glint of greed in her eyes remained the same as when she was the twisted old crone I first met centuries ago.

We'd been bound together for a long time now, thanks to our arrangement, even though each time I returned to her I would vow to myself that it would be the last time. But Cybilla always knew how to hook me back in like a desperate fish chasing that fat, juicy irresistible worm. Thanks to Cybilla's potions, a regular spray tan and some thick dark glasses, I was able to mask my physical appearance. This, combined with the years learning to manage my temper meant that I could now move freely within society without being shunned as a monster, or in fear of accidentally triggering my powers and turning people to stone.

But Cybilla's help came at a high price.

I dropped the coin onto the table with a thud.

"Well done, Medusa," she purred, lifting the ancient coin up to her face. "Remember this one?"

"Mithradates IV," I murmured.

"That's the one," she chuckled. "He was so afraid of death, constantly stuffing himself full of those horrible herbs to become immune to poisons. When all it took in the end was one look from my favourite Gorgon," she chuckled as she examined the coin, front and back.

"Do you have my payment?" I shifted in my seat, trying not to remember the last moments of Mithradates and all those came after him – that final look of terror, etched forever on their faces as they met my gaze.

"Of course, darling, here." She unclipped her handbag.

My heart thumped in anticipation as she pulled out a small red glass vial and held it out to me. I almost snatched it out of her hand in my haste, snapping it open to drink the bitter serum inside. A sensation of cold moved down my throat, freezing my human appearance in place as the potion made its way through my bloodstream.

As soon as I was able to move again, I stood to leave, not wanting to spend any more time with her than I had to.

"Before you go, there's one more thing," she said, slowly. "Sadly, Silphion – the herb which is a vital ingredient of your serum – is no longer available, gone extinct I hear. This means I can't make your potion anymore."

I nudged my sunglasses down a fraction and stared at her without saying a word, watching the look of panic cross her face as she quickly turned her eyes away from me to busy herself on her phone. "That is sad indeed. But maybe it's for the best? Maybe it's time for me to accept myself as I am."

"Oh no! That wasn't what I was going to suggest at all!" She let out an unnecessarily loud laugh, and a few people near us turned to look as she shook her head at me. "I've found something much better for you."

Behind my oversized sunglasses, I narrowed my eyes and waited as she slowly took a long drink of her coffee, then neatly lined her teaspoon back on the saucer before continuing.

"I've been researching how to help you, and came across the most wonderful spell. One that might actually be able to change you back to your beautiful old self, permanently. No more snake hair. No more stoney powers."

"Who do you want me to kill this time?" I whispered. If there was a permanent physical reversal, why was Cybilla telling me about it now? Was this another one of her tricks?

"Oh Medusa, you make it sound like *I'm* the monster here! Don't worry, you won't have to kill anyone. In fact, I think you're going to enjoy your next expedition. All you need to do is find a god or goddess and convince them to give you a drop of their blood."

"The gods have left this world, you know that."

"The pure gods have left, yes. So, sadly you've lost the chance to convince your maker Athena to part with her blood, but I have it on very good authority that some of the demi-gods are still around," she said while continuing to scroll through her phone, "not that they're easy to find. In fact, one of the only ones I've managed to track down lives here. You'll find a face you know holed up in this little piece of paradise." She slid her phone across the table. Flashing on the phone's screen was an advertisement for a holiday destination. It looked to be an island somewhere in the Mediterranean. Honeycombed sandstone cliffs crowding around gleaming turquoise pools, which looked like they were lit from within by the gleaming bodies of a thousand oceanids. I looked up at Cybilla, confused.

"Circe?" I asked, confused.

She tutted and shook her head. "Try a bit closer to home?" She tapped on the name of the island. Seriphos.

"Perseus?" I whispered. "But… he died?"

"He lives, my dear. Demi-gods are not easily got rid of."

Perseus was alive. This was unexpected news. The last time I had seen Perseus all those years ago, he'd been sent to kill me but had showed mercy instead, and ever since our stories had become intertwined through the course of history. I didn't particularly want to find out how he felt about me now, after all these years; but if there was the smallest hope that he could help me, I had to take the chance.

"What do I need to do?" I asked.

"Find him, and convince him to give you a few drops of his blood. A potion created using divine blood can make the effects of your change permanent. He's your best chance, I'm afraid – if you want a new potion in time."

I pursed my lips and looked her straight in the eye. She clearly didn't know Perseus's parting words to me. He'd spared me but said that, if our paths were to ever cross again, he would finish what he had set out to do. Time may have softened that resolve. Time may also have hardened it, especially if he knew what I had become, a killer and thief for hire.

Either way, if it meant having my old life back, being human again, it was worth the risk.

As long as the cost wasn't just as great… "And what will this deal cost me?" Cybilla never did anything out of kindness.

"Don't fret about that for now, we'll work it out later…" She smiled her crooked smile, hooked her bag under her arm, and sashayed out of the café before I could say another word.

From where I stood, the island of Seriphos seemed little changed since the time of the gods. Down by the water's edge, yes, the marina and the ceaseless crawl of buildings up into the hillside had transformed the island; but up here, away from the bustle of the tourists and tavernas of the main town, it felt like I had stepped back to the days when I was still human.

I took my tiny rental car up the precarious goat track of a road as far as I could, before pulling up to the side of this tiny roadside taverna. A few tourists sat around enjoying the cool shade provided by the building, tucking into gyros and chips, and cold beers. I took the last free table and sat down, ordering a small meal of fresh dolmadakia and saganakis made of the local cheese, more to put off what I was here to do than to sate my appetite.

The wrinkled old woman who brought out my meal took one look at me and thumped my plate on the table before hurrying away, making the sign of the cross across her chest. What did she know that I didn't?

I finished my meal and set off on foot towards a small white building in the distance, passing the same gnarled and wind-moulded trees clinging to the threadbare soils as would have stood here when the gods walked on the island.

What if Perseus changed his mind and finished the job with which he was initially tasked?

All too soon I was at the house and stood frozen at the front gate. He had spared my life once, yes, but his parting threat was still fresh in my mind. Too late to turn back now. I exhaled and lifted the latch to push the gate open.

I almost expected a bolt of lightning to lash down from the cloudless sky and incinerate me on the spot, or a hound of hell to bowl me over and tear me to pieces. But nothing happened as I walked towards the house, willing one step in front of the other. The Perseus I remembered was a feared warrior, but all around me were the signs of different labours. Silvery olive trees, laden with jade green fruit lined the path down to the house, beyond which were rows of green, flashes of yellow lemons, scarlet pomegranates bobbing against the breeze. Vivid green grapevines were trained to grow along the front wall of the house, which sheltered them from the gusty ocean breeze.

The front door swung open before I had the chance to knock and there he stood. The years had etched signs of age on his face. His eyes were more hooded than I remembered, pushed down by the years spent outdoors, and deep lines ran across his once smooth forehead. But he still stood tall, his former cocky assuredness somewhat mellowed.

"Medusa." His gravelly voice brought me back to the present.

I cleared my throat. "Can I come in?" I felt like I was talking through water, each word an effort to enunciate.

He moved aside without a word, and I stepped through the

door. I noticed that he kept his gaze down, careful not to look me in the eyes. Clearly he hadn't forgotten the source of my power.

The house was humble for someone who was a legend among men. There were more plants inside, adding splashes of green against stark white walls. The floorboards were covered with thick mats, on top of which sat simple functional wooden furnishings. Displayed on the otherwise bare walls were the swords and knives of a once famous hero, and I could tell from the way they caught the light that they were kept sharp by their owner.

"Are you hungry?" He pointed me to a chair and walked out of sight.

I soon heard the scraping and clattering of dishes and clinking of glasses.

He returned with a plate piled with fruit, hard cheese and almonds, which he placed on the low table between us. "What brings the Gorgon to my door?" he asked, passing me a glass of water.

I took a long drink and slowly put the glass down on the table, careful not to let my hand tremble. "As you can see, I look... different to the last time we met."

He nodded, saying nothing, forcing me to fill the silence with more words.

"I... I've been able to mask the effects of the curse." I stretched my arms out to demonstrate my normal appearance.

"And what about your power? Can you still turn any creature into a garden ornament?"

"I can," I said slowly, "I've learnt to control my temper, so it only happens when I desire it."

"And have you come here to turn me to stone?" he asked, his eyes narrowing as he spoke.

I shook my head quickly. "No. No I've sought you out because I need your help."

He reached for a handful of almonds before leaning back into his chair, waiting for me to continue.

"Do you remember Cybilla the witch?"

He jutted his lips out and slowly shook his head. "Never heard of her."

"Cybilla makes a potion for me, a salve that masks my appearance and helps me blend in," I said. "But the effects are temporary, and in repayment I must... retrieve items for her – magical amulets, priceless objects that still hold traces of power from the time of the gods, the kinds of objects that their owners aren't exactly happy to give up."

"So, you're a thief?" he bit into a slice of apple he spoke.

"I'm a... I'm a thief, yes. And worse," I whispered with a wince, watching his face.

"If you don't like her, why don't you kill her and just be yourself?" he asked casually, picking at a piece of cheese.

"Because she gives me what I need to exist in this world, among other people, without being afraid, or feared." I said finally.

"But you are the fearsome Medusa. Or have you forgotten who you are?" he asked with a small smile.

I blew out a breath. I must sound like a weak petulant child to him. The mighty self-assured Perseus, living here in this blue-skied paradise, growing his own food, making his own wine, freshly cut roses from his garden to perfume his home. And here I was, a mopey remnant from his past here to seek his help. Maybe Cybilla had sent me here as some kind of sick punishment, to remind me how powerless and pathetic I had become, nothing more than her beast on a chain that she yanked to do her bidding.

"Why are you so afraid of being alone? I'm alone here and couldn't be happier. People like you and me, we're not like the rest of them down there." He pointed a finger down towards the village.

"You're alone because you choose to be, not because you're forced to," I whispered. "I've lived most of my life hiding, in fear of being feared." I hesitated before continuing. I hadn't thought through what would happen if Perseus refused to give me what I wanted, and now that I was here, I wanted to get away as quickly as possible. "There's a way that the effects of Cybilla's potion can be made permanent. But it needs some blood of a god, or demi-god, willingly given."

I waited for him to fly up and behead me where I sat; instead, he sat silent, staring out the window for so long that I thought he had turned to stone.

"Are we talking a few drops, or do I need to be completely drained?" he said, finally.

"A few drops is all I need," I laughed in relief as I rifled through my bag for the thimble-sized vial Cybilla had given me. I handed it over to him.

"I'll do this for you, but then we're done. I've left my past behind, and don't want it to seek me out again."

I nodded. Perseus was being a good host, yes, but I had not forgotten how quickly he could turn. He picked up the knife he must have used earlier to slice the apple and used it to pierce the tip of his index finger, squeezing to draw out a small dome of blood without the slightest change of expression. He carefully transferred the liquid into the vial before sealing it back up.

"Thank you, Perseus. This is incredibly generous of you."

"Let's call it even for the time I tried to kill you. And," he added, handing the vial back, "I guess you won't need Cybilla any more after this."

"That right." I carefully wrapped it in my silk scarf, placed it back in my bag and stood to leave. "I'll never have to see her again. I can just walk away." As I said the words, I realised Cybilla would never let that happen. I knew too much about her, her business and operations. I would always be a threat to her. Even now, she was probably plotting a way to keep me under her control. The only way I would be free was to rid myself of her forever.

The gleam of the table in front of me caught my eye as I stood, and a lost memory bubbled up to the surface of my mind. "Do you still have the mirror you used when you came to my cave?"

He furrowed his brows for a moment, before giving a small nod. "Give me a minute," he said as he rose and walked out of the room. He returned with a small wooden box and kneeled on the floor to place it on the table between us, rubbing away the thick layer of dust encrusted on the top before pushing the lid open.

"Take it, I have no use for this." He held up the small round item of polished silver.

I held my breath as I took the mirror from him, running my thumb against its cool smooth surface. I could see myself reflected on its surface, the real me with my snaky hair, normally masked by Cybilla's enchantment. "Athena's mirror," I breathed.

Cybilla had always been cunning enough to avoid looking at me directly whenever I met with her, protecting herself with spells that I could never penetrate.

But with Athena's mirror, enchanted by the goddess herself, I could slip past her guard, after she helped me one final time.

I was back in our usual café, where we met after every mission, Cybilla facing the sun, me with my back to the window.

"This took longer than expected but I've done it," she exclaimed as she handed me a small, gift-wrapped parcel.

"It worked?" I took the parcel from her and carefully tore it open. Inside, wrapped in layers of tissues, was a small black vial. I snapped it open and sniffed the contents.

"Go on, drink it quick before the air spoils it! Then let's talk business, there's something I need you to do for me."

I knew it – there would always be another job, another scheme. "Before I do, I have something for you, a thank-you gift," I said, careful not to spill my precious potion as I reached over into my bag and pulled out my gift, wrapped for her in a red scarf, her favourite colour. "When I was with Perseus, I found this hidden away in an old trunk that he had in his home, crammed full of the most incredible treasures," I said, watching her eyes light up.

"You stole it for me?" she whispered, the familiar crooked smile creeping across her face.

I nodded slowly, as I pushed the parcel across the table toward her. The only way to distract her into dropping her guard was by exploiting her greed. "It's very valuable, which is why I thought you'd like to have it."

She unwrapped it cautiously, using the back of her spoon to push back the layers of red silk until she stopped and, with a gasp, held the mirror up to her face. "It's the most beautiful thing I've ever seen," she breathed, her gaze trapped by the enchanted mirror.

"It can be." I slipped my sunglasses off and angled myself so that I could look into her eyes through the mirror.

The last thing she uttered was the usual surprised intake of breath made by Medusa's victims, cut off halfway as her throat turned to stone.

I tipped my head back and swallowed the contents of the vial. It tasted hot, and burned as it travelled down my throat. I coughed and gulped down a glass of water to help soothe the pain.

The burning sensation passed quickly, leaving a warmness to bloom out from my centre and spread across my body, until even my fingertips tingled with energy. It had worked, I could feel it. I held my hand up to look at my pink fingertips, marvelling at the quality of the enchantment. "It's worked!" I laughed out loud. I looked human again, completely human.

"Thank you," I whispered to Cybilla as I snapped her fingers off Athena's mirror.

I was about to drop it into my bag when something caught my eye. Instead, I tipped the contents of my bag, including the mirror, into Cybilla's shiny red snake-skin bag, Cybilla had no need for it anymore, and the old Medusa always did look good in red. I hooked my new possession into the crook of my arm and sashayed out the café.

ABOUT 'STONE HEARTED'

The stories of myth and legend created so many typical 'monster' archetypes that I wanted to examine this through a contemporary lens. 'Stone Hearted' is thus a 'what if' take on the old story of Perseus slaying Medusa in order to save his mother. What if Perseus had chosen to be merciful and didn't kill Medusa? As an immortal, Medusa would have had to use her resourcefulness and adapt to surviving within a changing world. The symbology associated with this archetype are that of rage, shame and envy, and in this retelling Medusa has learnt to forgive her abusers and also herself. My inspiration was to explore the perspective of a villain who is also a victim, and the choices she makes to move beyond either label.

ABOUT A.R KELLY

A R Kelly is a Northern Beaches local who writes stories that explore our interactions with technology and imagines realities where science and magic merge into one. She has published a number of short stories and is working on her first novel.

AVENGEMENT

———⌁———

SUSAN STEGGALL

Jehanne clutches my arm as she walks to her fate. She is barefoot and dressed in a simple tunic. A mitred paper cap on her head bears the clumsily written words: heretic, liar, a disgrace to country, faith and womanhood. The crowd kneels in silence as we climb steps to a platform where the executioner is waiting next to a large pyre. He uses heavy chains to attach her shoulders, waist and knees to a tall wooden stake. He picks up a smouldering braise of resin and puts it to the pile of logs.

Tongues of flame lick my priest's robes. Jehanne orders me away. Then the blaze roars up. In a faltering voice, she cries: "My Voices truly came from God!" A cloud of black smoke billows from the column of fire. She screams, "Jesus... Jesu... Je..." before her head is engulfed in the inferno.

The conflagration subsides for an instant, revealing a naked corpse, red and black, twisted in an atrocious death. The flesh explodes. The spectacle collapses. The fire has done its work.

Brother Martin leans against Saint Sauveur Church unable to move from the horror, shaken to the core of his being. The smell of burning flesh, the pain in hands scorched by the flames, Jehanne's anguished cries, the triumphant shouts of her executioners – will stay with him forever. It is only when he is prodded by an English lance that he rouses enough to leave Rouen's marketplace, his faith crumbling with each faltering step. If the bishop and his acolytes are the public face of the day's villainy, Martin's lack of courage in speaking up for Jehanne will haunt him without mercy.

At the priory, he goes in search of the labourer who works in the vegetable patch and offers the man his silver cross and priest's clothing in exchange for peasant breeches and jacket. The man agrees: he can get good money for the silver and his wife will be very happy with the cloth. Martin returns to his cell for the last time to retrieve an old letter – the only thing he has of his parents. He doesn't even know if they or his siblings are alive. In any case he would be ashamed to admit to them his failure to save Jehanne. He passes by the kitchens for some rough bread and hard cheese. He also takes a knife and a strike-a-light iron and its flint, then sets out to seek solace in the countryside.

He wanders far and wide, dodging marauding bands, renegade Frenchmen and desperate English soldiers. Everywhere he finds villages destroyed, crops ravaged, fountains smashed. He slakes his thirst in rippling streams. In one ruined field he finds a few carrots; in a broken orchard some overripe apples. He cuts rotting flesh off a dead goat and makes a meagre fire to cook the rancid meat. He offers his services to farmers struggling to rebuild their livelihoods. Martin is young and strong and, although the first few weeks of backbreaking labour are harder than anything he has ever done, he is soon in demand as a willing pair of hands.

After six years on the fringes of a rural France in tatters, Martin arrives at Domremy, the village where Jehanne had been born in 1412, near the left bank of the River Meuse. He has come to honour his promise to tell Jehanne's parents of her unwavering love for them. He sits on the stump of an old beech tree to recall what she told him of her childhood.

In her father's garden, she minded the chickens, ducks and turkeys, and took the goats and sheep to pasture. Her mother taught her to spin, and by the age of eight she was reputedly the best weaver in Domremy. Very early, Jehanne showed an intense level of piety, practising the sacrament, taking alms to the poor. On the edge of the village was an ancient wood, *Le Bois Chenu*, and at its entrance a majestic beech tree. In Spring, Jehanne, like all young people in the village, enjoyed picnics under the tree's spreading branches and danced around it on fete days.

Martin runs his hands over the rough surface of the broken tree as if to invoke those happy times. At the sound of voices, he looks up to see two people emerge from a nearby barn; a man holding a long scythe and a woman with a basket on her arm. They stare at Martin. After a few minutes the man advances several paces then stops, alert, suspicious, the metal blade of the scythe glinting in the sun.

The woman puts down her basket, walks slowly towards Martin and stands in front of him. "Good day, *M'sieur*. I haven't seen you in these parts before. Who are you and where are you from?" she asks, her tone curious rather than confronting.

"My name is Martin. I am…" He hesitates about revealing more of his story, but encouraged by the woman's friendly expression, he decides to confide in her. "I come, originally, from Rouen."

"Ah… Rouen. Are you here about Jehanne?"

"Yes, to…"

The woman cuts him off. "I was her closest friend. I am Mengette, and he," she says, pointing to the watchful man, is Jean, my husband." She makes a 'thumbs up' sign to her husband that there is no danger. He heads towards a field of long grass next to the barn but, instead of beginning to reap, he lingers near the fence. She turns back to Martin. "So, why exactly have you come?"

"I was hoping to find out more of her life before… she…"

Mengette bends down, tears off a blade of grass and chews on it. "It's a long story. Do you have time?"

"All the time in the world."

"Well…" Mengette appears to choose her words carefully. "When we were thirteen years old, a cloud of angels dressed in white appeared to Jehanne and a voice called her by name. She knew her family would never believe her, so she stayed silent. At first she didn't even tell me. Several days later the angels came again to tell her she would command an army. Saint Catherine and Saint Margaret appeared to her too. She tried to tell her family, but her father would not listen. This troubled her greatly, but the saints continued to appear. She was guarding a flock of ewes on that very hill," Mengette points in the direction from which Martin had come, "when, she said, a heavenly voice told her she'd been chosen to restore the kingdom of France."

"She talked to me about her Voices too." Martin says.

Mengette puts a hand over her heart in agreement. "She knew France was in danger, but no one would listen to a peasant woman. Then the roads became unsafe. Men ravaged the countryside, setting fire to houses and barns, taking everything they could steal, even from churches. We were warned not to talk to anyone, even neighbours – there were spies everywhere. No one was safe." Mengette's voice falters.

Martin tries to comfort her. "It was a truly terrible time. The English army occupied so many of our regions. I assume you all knew that Charles VII was no longer king of France?'

'Yes. Jehanne's father was a farmer like the rest of us but he was also a village councillor and attended meetings on Domremy's behalf, in the regional centre of Coussey. That's where he learned about the English king, Henry VI, wearing two crowns – his own and ours." She picks up a stick and draws a rough coat-of-arms consisting of a bow and three crossed arrows in the dirt. "The d'Arc family coat-of-arms," Mengette says, "but it didn't protect us. We had to pay a ransom of two hundred gold écus to save

Domremy, but the soldiers still flattened our crops and destroyed our windmills. There was nothing we could do – all we had were farm tools. And Jehanne." She looks directly at Martin. "She was the only one with the courage to take on the enemy."

"Are her parents still alive?"

Mengette's expression falls. "Her mother, Isabelle Romée, is very much in this world. But her father, Jacques d'Arc…" She takes a deep breath. "He died shortly after hawkers brought news of Jehanne's execution. Although he was strict, he loved her greatly. They say he died of chagrin."

"One more death to bear," Martin whispers. "Why did Jehanne want to meet Captain Baudricourt at the Fortress Vaucouleurs?"

"Because he was our overlord and a man of much influence. By 1428, our situation was so desperate Jehanne convinced her cousin, Durand Laxart, to accompany her to the fortress to persuade Baudricourt to take her before King Charles. But of course, such an important man was not going to consult with a mere girl. She persisted and finally obtained a meeting with the captain. Dressed in full chainmail, with a sword at his side, I imagine he cut a fearfully impressive figure. But Jehanne held her nerve and insisted *she* would lead King Charles to his consecration, though not until the following year. Robert de Baudricourt thought her ridiculous, so she told me later."

Mengette stops speaking to sip water from a leather gourd at her waist. She offers some to Martin before continuing.

"Meanwhile renegade Burgundian troops were marching

closer to Domremy. We gathered our remaining herds and possessions, and fled to Neufchâtel."

"You would have been safe there."

She nods. "We were there for fifteen days before news came that the soldiers had moved on. I'll never forget the journey home, the thick smoke along the way, the wheatfields and houses burned to the ground. Our church and its tower," she gestures towards the ruins, "were heaps of ash, the tombs in the cemetery desecrated, this great beech tree chopped down." Mengette pats the stump, then looks suspiciously at Martin. "So what is your connection to Jehanne?"

"I was with her, when she died," he replies in a low voice.

The woman takes a deep breath as if to gather up her courage. "Then you must tell me what happened, please."

"It was truly terrible. I will spare you the worst."

"Spare me nothing!"

Martin begins by describing to Mengette Jehanne's refusal to sign the false documents, which led to her incarceration in the Duke of Warwick's château instead of, as promised, being sent to a church prison. "Her guards tormented her constantly," Martin says. "She had been deceived by those in high office, particularly the French clergy. Then came the final day…" When Martin comes to the moment the flames flared up, he stops speaking, reliving the terrible scene – an inferno straight from Hell. "The stench of burnt flesh filled the air," he whispers. "The English scattered her ashes in the river."

"Perhaps for the best." Mengette's turn to comfort Martin.

"When I returned to my priory in Rouen, a tremendous sadness overcame me," Martin says. "I set out to look for traces of Jehanne – visiting places that were important to her. As I followed the route of her victories and defeats, I took some consolation in the murmur of the river, the singing of birds and the early morning mists. I wish now that I had believed her from the start."

"Why didn't you?"

He shakes his head. "The laws they used to accuse her were… complicated and obscure. I didn't have the legal training to understand them properly, so I thought her sentence just, at the time."

Mengette frowns, angry. "And now? Do you still find her sentence just?"

Martin puts his head in his hands and whispers, "No."

"Well then," Mengette replies, "you must avenge her death, or your soul will rot in hell. I am a married woman with family duties." She glances towards her husband. "You will have to do this alone."

Martin closes his eyes, seeing in his mind the many roads he is yet to travel, with all their hardships and dangers.

Mengette shakes him. "Come now, who bore the greatest responsibility?"

"The bishop," Martin says, "Pierre Cauchon, Bishop of Beauvais. The English promised him the archbishopric of Rouen if he arranged for Jehanne's dishonour. People may say he is a renowned liberal arts scholar, but he is a venal, cunning man, who puts personal advancement above any human suffering or pastoral care. So, he had the English invaders and their French vassals subject Jehanne to ignominy, insults, trickery and treachery. They threatened her with so much physical and psychological torture she no longer knew whom to trust. She resisted as long as she could." Martin looks down at his calloused toes in threadbare sandals, thinking of the clattering of ironclad soldiers' feet on the paving stones of Rouen on that fateful day. "Cauchon had Jehanne tricked into putting on men's clothes again, and it was on that flimsy pretext she was finally condemned."

"I will need proof," Mengette says in a hard voice. "You must return with proof that he is dead."

Martin nods, his mind now clear.

Martin's search takes him through silent and sombre lands that seem to be permanently in winter – frost on the trees, fruit shrivelled on the vine, crops dead in the fields. Each time he climbs a hill he meets snow. It is as if an ice age is coming over the land. The snowline moves lower with the seasonal cold; glaciers are advancing, overrunning farms at higher altitudes. There is widespread crop failure. The price of grain increases; wine is already difficult to produce. Starvation and poverty loom for many people far and wide. Martin is cold and hungry most of the time, yet endures it without complaint; it is his penance for being so weak of spirit.

At a convent, where he shelters from a snowstorm, he learns

that Bishop Cauchon has not been granted the bishopric of Rouen, which he so ardently desired. He has been demoted and transferred to the seat of Lisieux, to the west, many leagues away, through hostile country.

Martin trudges on. Occasionally he seeks work in the fields in exchange for food. When his clothes are almost in rags, a farmer's wife takes pity on him and asks her husband to employ him to guard their sheep against wolves.

It takes Martin almost five years to reach Lisieux, a town still in English hands. He finds lodgings with a family in exchange for helping repair their barn, damaged in a fierce storm. Discretely he makes enquiries about Bishop Cauchon. With each questioning, he receives furtive looks and evasive replies. In an *auberge* he buys a hot wine and listens attentively to the gossip. He hears a man say that the bishop is unwell with a strange disease and is no longer seen in public. It heartens Martin to learn how unpopular Bishop Cauchon has become.

It is already December when Martin inveigles his way into the bishop's residence. Finding the prelate's private quarters in the vast building is difficult but, remembering Jehanne's determination, Martin succeeds. For several days he watches the bishop's heavily guarded first-floor bedchamber, from a hiding place in a nearby storeroom. One day, luck is with him. The guards depart *en masse*, leaving the door unlocked. Martin seizes his chance and slips inside.

The room is dark and airless, all windows closed, all curtains drawn. There is something sinister in the atmosphere too. Martin recognises it as the smell of decay and death. At the sound of moaning, he creeps towards a huge bedstead for the source of the inhuman sound. He moves nearer to find a pitiful human wreck, his face a hideous grotesquerie.

"Bishop Cauchon, you knew Jehanne was innocent. You sent her to her death. Why?" Martin demands harshly.

The figure in the bed struggles to sit up. Martin sees a man old beyond his years, reduced to a miserable bundle of bones by a cankerous growth eating away at his mouth and tongue. The bishop tries to speak, but only animal sounds emerge from his disease-ravaged face.

Martin realises then that he will never hear from Pierre Cauchon's lips why Jehanne had to be put to death. His murderous rage subsides. He would be no better than those who betrayed and executed her if he tortured and killed this feeble ailing man. He remembers Cauchon's final words to Jehanne and smiles at the irony in them: "We pronounce that you, a rotten limb from whom infection could invade other limbs, must be rejected and removed from the body of the Church." It could be the bishop's own epitaph – and God's vengeance. The affliction that has befallen Cauchon has removed from his body the very 'limb' that served him so profitably all his life – the faculty of speech.

Voices approach. Martin hides behind a heavy wall tapestry. Two men whom he recognises from the medical fraternity enter and stand by the bed, murmuring between themselves as they watch the bishop through his last hours. When his rasping breathing stops, they close the dead man's eyes and leave the room.

Martin sidles up to the bed, gagging at the gangrenous stink pervading the air. He picks up a set of silver tongs from a nearby table and carefully removes a blackened tooth from the bishop's crumbling jawbone. On the same table he sees a parchment. It is an absolution from Pope Eugene who, from the tenor of his words, was well aware of Cauchon's part in Jehanne's execution, even praising the bishop for it. Martin wraps the tooth in the parchment and puts it in his travel-worn satchel to take back to Mengette.

At the sound of loud footsteps on the flagstones in the hallway, he climbs onto the windowsill, slides to the ground, and steals away. That night, for the first time in years, when Martin closes his eyes, the flames are no longer there.

ABOUT 'AVENGEMENT'

'Avengement', based on the life of Saint Joan of Arc, is an exploration of how politics and religion can join forces with tragic consequences. If 'Jehanne' has been declared a hero, there were many villains in her story: the kings of England and France, their royal courts and army commanders. The Church and the French legal fraternity were also culpable. Perhaps the dubious honour of 'arch villain' belonged to Bishop Pierre Cauchon, who sought advancement through noble patronage, which meant currying favour with his English overlords; he stooped low to achieve that end. In the tumultuous first half of the fifteenth century, Jehanne's religious fervour provoked a fanatical zeal on the part of those in power to crush her, a villainous act etched in the annals of history.

After lifting the siege of Orléans in 1429, Jehanne defeated the turncoat French and their English allies in several significant battles. At Compiègne in 1430, she was captured by Burgundian forces and sold to England for ten thousand pounds in gold. She was judged a witch, her voices the work of the devil. A pro-English court found her guilty of heresy and she was burned at the stake on 30 May 1431. In 1455, Pope Calixte III constituted a tribunal to revisit the trial. The result, pronounced on 7 July 1456, exonerated Jehanne, finding the original judgement was influenced by iniquity, bad faith, errors of fact and law. Jehanne became a national hero, her memory honoured every year on 8 May, which is the anniversary of her deliverance of Orléans. This date also celebrates her beatification in 1909 and canonisation in 1920.

The location of Pierre Cauchon's burial site was unclear until his skeleton was discovered during renovations in Lisieux Cathedral in 1931. The official version of his death was cardiac failure; for Brother Martin it was a failure of heart. Cauchon was later reburied, without ceremony or salvation, but since no identification was added, the whereabouts of this principal villain in Jehanne's story remains unknown.

To this day, no one understands Jehanne's Voices; but without them she would not have made her mark on history. She was, and will remain, according to Philippe de Villiers, the purest work of art that an allegorical spirit has ever inserted into our literature.

ADDITIONAL SOURCES

The opening scene was translated and adapted from Philippe de Villiers, *Le Roman de Jeanne d'Arc*, (Albin Michel, 2014). Many of the historical facts have been taken from *Les Grands Noms de l'Histoire: Jeanne d'Arc*, Editions du Rocher, 1998.

ABOUT SUSAN STEGGALL

Susan Steggall has written: *Alpine Beach: A Family Adventure* (1999); a family history series; a biography, *A Most Generous Scholar: Joan Kerr, Art and Architectural Historian* (a successful PhD thesis and a non-fiction winner in the 2013 Society of Women Writers NSW (SWW) Book Awards); novels: *Forget Me Not* (2006), *It Happened Tomorrow* (2013), *'Tis the Doing Not the Deed* (2019) and *The Heritage You Leave Behind* (2021), which was Highly Commended in the SWW 2022 Book Awards. Susan also writes art-related articles, exhibition and book reviews, book chapters and essays.

A BLOODIED TAIL

———cℵɔ———

ZENA SHAPTER

Water darkens as if rainclouds swell high above the ocean surface. Deepening shadows dull the sunlit arches that open my underwater hollow to the sea, dim the sandy floor and curving rock walls of my home, and scare a harem of yellow sea goldies from swimming around the tins and bowls on my shelves. They dash inside the old dinghy where I sleep, while I swish outside and glance up. But… the sky is clear. An innocent pale blue gleams. Occasional white clouds drift. The sea should be its usual glimmering aqua. Instead a dark navy spreads through the water and reaches for me, which can only mean one thing. He already knows what I've done. I should never have told my daughter the truth.

I surface to judge how long I have. Along the shore, humans haul dinghies and canoes to wedge them between coconut trees, shielding eyes from the sun as they stare out to sea, confused. They can't see it, but they feel it – a storm is on its way, and it's coming in fast. Gentle breezes that moments ago caressed palm fronds with seahorse grace, now bluster as sand blasts to sting their supple skin. A cool water current swirls towards the land and shivers my shoulders too. Scales in my tail prickle with warning. Creases in the sand beneath me deepen, as if bowing before the force of nature approaching.

I flip down to draw my woven kelp panels over each arched opening. More out of habit than hope. When real storms lash and cry, the panels are enough to keep me snug and secure. But the ocean only turns this vivid periwinkle tint when Triton is angry, and I won't wait here to receive it. Doors hooked in place, I swim for the lagoon where he'll never go. Too shallow for most merfolk, his bulk will bulge above it, and he won't break his own commandment: to never be seen.

Behind me, the yellow goldies try to keep up, then turn and dash for the headland reef instead. It's closer, but he's found me there before, in the first weeks after we separated, when we still clashed over how to raise our daughters. It's been easier since I accepted I no longer have a say. My choices set me in the current that brought me here, so here I must stay. Besides, Triton is our king. With no ordinary marriage, ours can be no ordinary estrangement.

"Seyla!" he bellows through the water as he nears. "I warned you!"

I reach the lagoon, hide behind its sandbar, flatten myself among the soft grains, then dig a small trough through which to watch him. The water itself seems to still in fear of him.

"I forbade you!" he booms. "Yet you filled her head with your nonsense!"

I bite my tongue. Nonsense is subjective. What mother wouldn't try to cheer her child when they cry?

"A human soul is worth nothing of our 300 years!" Triton swishes to a stop before my rocky outcrop. The power of his wake flings my kelp panels aside. He lowers his head, leaning on his trident to glare inside my hollow. The frown on his forehead deepens as he judges how I live; no doubt condemning all the experiments and concoctions I left on my benchtop.

Yes, I'm still researching. What business is it of his? I keep myself to myself, as he insisted. My daughter came to find me.

"Seyla!" he roars, sending violent ripples through the water.

He waits for a response, his bare chest hard and muscled, his black opal tail as thick and mighty as the toughest merman under his command. His long beard, though, drifting like a pointed seagrass clump – is greyer than I remember. How long has it been since I've seen him? When I want to see our daughters I keep to the kelp forest, staying cloaked in the swaying masses, hidden from any court official accompanying them. But Triton rarely leaves the city.

"Seyla!" He straightens and searches around.

I duck back down.

"You'll never see her again!" He's said the same before, of all our daughters. "And I'll not change my mind!"

But his taunts mean nothing to me anymore. I'm not coming out.

He's silent a moment, accepting it, then a rushing whirl of water almost blasts me backwards – him swimming away.

I wait until the flux dissipates, then peek over the sandbar. He's gone. The water brightens. Sunbeams spiral gently through the turquoise. A school of silvery grey threadfin edge slowly past like they're still scared. They needn't be. I show them by clawing over the sand with a smile, then gliding back down to my hollow.

My smile fades. My kelp panels are ripped and floating in snapped weaves. Debris drifts out from under each arch, the force of Triton's wake having smashed my coral utensils, shell bowls, and the lidded glass jars that protect my experiments. I sink as I calculate all the work I'll have to do again. He meant to do this.

I gather what fragments I can into a carved tortoiseshell platter – once a prized wedding gift, now cracked and chipped. Still, it's my daughters I pity; their vibrant minds stifled under his constant wrathful control. I stare towards the city, shrouded by the vast oceans of my childhood, where I too once danced, giggled and glided idly, as my many daughters do now; not knowing I was confined to a path of performance, that my life would never really be my own. I can almost hear the music and laughter – all lost to me the moment I gave birth and realised the bleak fragility of merlife.

'Humans never die,' I sobbed to Triton while cradling our first-born, 'they live forever.'

'What nonsense!' he laughed even then, amused.

'They ate a fruit from a mythical garden. It gave them eternal souls.'

'Then my men shall search the farthest reefs and forests of the sea. They will bring you every strange fruit they find and you too shall have a soul.' How I loved him for his kindness.

But with each daughter, I found less and less time to test the fruits on sea creatures, monitor their reactions, or log their sudden poisoned deaths. I planted seeds and strange flora grew, ready for when I could complete my studies. I snatched hours here and there to theorise, etch notes and design trials, but needed more time. I was doing it for my children. For all merfolk.

Yet when Triton commanded 'no more', and I begged to continue, no one spoke up for me. My daughters all turned their backs, resentful. They claimed there was nothing wrong with dancing as sea foam when they died.

They're wrong of course, and I'll prove it to them.

I drop the platter and swish inside to where all my test compotes are buried, under my dinghy's bow. My latest compote hasn't harmed any creatures, but I'll never know if anything actually works unless I try it myself, see how it feels.

The sand is uneven from Triton's wake, but the compote should be between the two blue bottles I buried with it.

I move the sand forward and back, left and right, but... it's gone. "Triton!" I mutter. He must have taken it. I roll my lips. This time he's gone too far. "This is beyond..."

"Seyla!" sings a voice as slight as a newborn jellyfish.

The light outside seems to radiate, glowing with a luminosity that can only reflect off a princess's jewels.

I glide outside and gasp. My daughters are as beautiful as sirens. All of them bejewelled in precious necklaces and bangles, encrusted with pearls and polished glass gems. Fine long hair of every colour drifts around them cloud-like and serene.

No, not all of them. Not my youngest, Lea.

Tyna, my eldest, glides forward, her wavy blue-silver locks draped over a shoulder. "Did you give it to her?" her tone not quite an accusation.

"Give what to who?" I want to whirl among them and hold them to me.

"Your potion. Father said it was you."

"My po…" I glance back into my hollow. When Lea was here yesterday, she was crying over some boy she just met, asking if gaining an eternal soul would make her human. And she was sitting in my dinghy… right at its bow. "*Lea* took it?"

"Yes, and now she's one of them." Tyna lets out a sob.

The others crowd around her, whimpering words like 'never coming home', 'disgusting legs', and 'can't even talk'.

I glide closer. "Slow down. Tell me what's happened."

"Father was so angry," Tyna's voice quivers as she explains, "that the two of you even spoke – you should have seen his rage–"

"I saw enough," I mumble.

"He caused a storm down the coast, so violent it caught a ship. The prince's ship."

58

"Whose?" I edge closer still.

"The *Prince*," Tyna repeats, as if that's enough to clarify. "Lea couldn't let him drown of course, so she saved him."

"Drown? The boy she likes is *human*?" I sneer.

"Yes! She swam him to a beach, heaved him up the sand – we all saw." The others nod. "But then more humans ran over and she didn't have time to make it back to the water." Tyna closes her eyes, presses her lips together like she's trying not to cry.

Lana, my second eldest, rubs Tyna's arm and whispers an encouragement, glaring at me through her black seaweed curls, flowing as a whirlwind of night.

Tyna nods to her, like she's ready to continue. "Our poor sister, she must have been so scared. The humans had swords and knives and nets... But she had *your* potion with her, so of course she drank it!"

Dreena swims to me then. She's barely a year older than Lea, yet looks at me with the wisdom of an elder. Her yellow-grey hair glimmers as the scales of a butterflyfish. "Mother, you must come now, and convince Father to change his mind."

"Yes," Tyna adds. "Lea only drank it because she thought they'd kill her, so why not try for an eternal *soul*?" She spits the word like it's mud. "Instead she grew legs!" She shudders.

They all do.

But... "She changed, physically?" I gasp, searching their eyes for confirmation. "My compote worked?" I glance back at my hollow. I must check my notes. Which fruit was it, from which ocean? If legs are the price merfolk must pay to live forever, it might be worth it. And Lea's done it for love. She made her own choice. She's free to live now as she pleases.

"Please, Mother," Dreena pleads, reaching to tug my arm.

Her touch fills me with a warmth I dare not remember for the ache it might bring, that it has been this long. For the love of my daughters, I would do anything. Still… "Your father won't listen to me."

"But he could use his trident, make her like us again. Please." Dreena tugs again.

"Show her," Lana snaps, folding her arms.

The others seem to know exactly what she means, because they herd around me, and usher me down the coast. They're so fast, but I keep pace, for they carry my heart with them. They have from the moment they were born. These women, these beauties, I made them. I want them to live forever!

Along the shore, a tall white-column temple appears on a hill. Below it, a sandy cove is smattered with shipwreck debris. Further out to sea, a broken hull has sunk its dead to the deep.

My daughters stop far enough from land to remain unseen, yet close enough to observe a crowd of humans sitting outside the temple, cheering and clapping as a lithe young woman with long rosy hair dances before them. She whirls around in a delicate blue dress, her arms gliding with the grace of a princess, though her legs are as unsteady as a newborn. To them she smiles, but a mother knows when her child's smile cloaks a grimace.

"Lea?" My voice catches to see her in pain. "If she's with the boy she loves, why is she so unhappy?"

"Because she's not *with* him," Lana snaps, sniping like a crab's pincers. "He's the dark one – with the girl in yellow."

As she speaks, a dark-haired young man stands, his clothes torn and still damp. He pats Lea on the head like a pet, then bows to a brunette dressed in yellow and offers her his hand for a dance.

Merfolk have the same custom when dancing, but merfolk would never dismiss a hero so coldly, pathetically. If Lea saved his life, and if he's a prince, he should reward her with the gratitude of a nation, herald her with a royal respect. She risked everything for him! Yet here he takes another girl in his arms and dances!

When Lea faces the ocean again, her eyes brim with tears.

They flood into me and send me swimming to the surface. I have to help her. I'll call out and beg her to come home. I'll take care of her, I'll fix everything...

My daughters grip my tail so hard they claw out a scale. "You mustn't be seen!" they chorus.

"But if she just comes home," I tell them. "If she apologises to your father–"

"She won't understand you," Dreena says dismally. "We tried before, but our words are formless above the surface. No water to carry them."

"We sound like whales," Tyna mutters, letting me go.

I shiver at the thought, as if from a cool current swirling inland. My tail prickles where raw skin now throbs instead of a scale. A shadow envelopes me, drowning me in the grief of my daughter being beyond reach, beyond help.

"Let this be a warning," booms a voice behind us, Triton's voice – the cool shadows and prickles were his. "Disobey me, and you will suffer."

But he can't mean for his own daughter to suffer? Not when he could save her?

I turn to face him, seething with a storm of my own. "You would condemn your own child, just to make a point?"

"A king's command is nothing without proof."

"She's your daughter!" I shake my head. When exactly did his kindness end? Was it all because of me, because of the time I spent with my work? "There must be a way to help her. Unless… Do you not care for her at all? Do you not care for *anyone*?"

He pushes back his shoulders, gripping his trident with a rage only I can spear in him. "You would know, *wife*, given how little you cared for your own daughters as they grew. For the sake of what? Legs? Would you have all your daughters deformed and speechless?"

Ripples in the water flurry over my skin. My daughters drifting away from me. Do they think I'm like their father, with powers as deep as the trenches?

He signals for them to swim to him, and they obey without hesitation. "Should we have that done to you perhaps – turned into a sea monster, tentacles instead of a tail, only a screech for a voice, sea snakes crawling all over you? History should record you that way at least, for future generations to shudder at the mere thought of you. They'll judge Lea for her choices too, for she made them herself," he bellows with such command it could sink an island. "Let its currents take her where they will, as yours have taken you." He leaves his bitter words with me, then turns and coasts away.

My daughters follow, because I've long earnt their easy dismissal.

But what I deserve or don't is irrelevant while Lea remains onshore and helpless. Merfolk never leave kin behind, and Lea is my daughter whether she has legs or tail.

Still, my family disappear into the murk of ocean, and the glint of my husband's trident in a sunbeam is the only understanding I find – because I don't need Triton to help Lea, I only need his three-pronged spear.

He could use his trident, Dreena said earlier, *make her like us again.*

She spoke of the legend that tells of Poseidon creating merfolk to serve him in the seas. Gifted the trident, our first king was granted the power to populate the oceans by transforming sailors and their passengers into merfolk and, if they declined that gift, merfolk into humans again – not that any did.

That was a long time ago of course. I've no way of knowing if the trident still carries that power, or how I might even use it. Lea could also have a soul right now, in that human body of hers. Should I even try to change her back?

I turn to watch her again. As the dancing music ends, the prince leads his yellow girl inside the temple. Bells ring out. Left outside, Lea stands gazing out to sea, her lips parted, tears flowing. She knows she's made a mistake. She wants to come home. When she drank my compote, she never knew it would give her legs, take away the essence of who she is – a woman of the water.

She will be of water again.

I turn and plunge after Triton, powering through the depths, the inbound currents, and the silvery flashing shoals of herring and tuna until I catch up to his stately glide. Triton would never allow his daughters to enter his city flustered or bedraggled. So, as the golden domes and arches of his gleaming domain emerge beyond the thick kelp forest, my daughters slow to smooth down their hair and readjust their jewels.

Perimeter guards straighten their silver spears and bow to my family's regal entrance; but I dive down the kelp's long leafy strands to the ocean floor. From there, as usual, I can see the palace itself, past its curving gold walls and luminescent lanterns, and into the open throne arena where Triton mandates his subjects. Since my banishment, I've never dared to swim beyond these rough brown leaves; but Triton will leave his trident beside his throne before going to check the oyster farms or lobster pots, maybe as far as the seaweed crops, and I need to be ready.

I slip out of the kelp, dip close to the sand and under a passing sea ray to keep out of sight until I'm past the palace. Enticed with a belly rub, the gentle ray follows me to the open arena where Triton's throne is surrounded by raised benches. I glide under the lower seats and wait.

My family approaches, though it's not Triton carrying his trident to its resting rack – it's Lana, and she sees me. While the rest of them glide on, she frowns as she struggles to understand why I'm there, then realisation has her glaring at the trident in her hands and opening her mouth to call out. Something stops her. A thought, an idea. She closes her lips, balances the trident in its rack, and swims away.

Lea can't wait for me to find my nerve. I simply swim out and snatch the weapon, then dash back under the lower seats, past the palace, and into the kelp. I have it. I weave with it through the forest, plunge among the tuna and herring, find an inbound current and let it carry me back to shore. I have it, and there is the temple. There is the prince. There is Lea.

But they're walking away, heading for a wharf on the other side of the hill, to a docked galleon waiting there. The yellow girl still holds the prince's hand. Lea casts flower petals before the couple. Cheering crowds follow behind. The prince has married the yellow girl, and even a human could see Lea's forced smile for what it is. Heartbreak.

But I have the trident, and my daughter is here, crossing the wharf now and onto the galleon. So I search the spear and each of its three teethed prongs for inscriptions or patterns, any indication of how to use it. The smooth metal glints as if laughing. Who am I to wield its power? The mere mother of a child deformed and despairing?

Yes. Exactly that. And all the rage of it is mine, all the injustice and the sodden tears that simply wash away in the seawater is mine, and I wish for Lea's choice to wash away with them. So as the galleon departs, I hold the trident outstretched and close my eyes, channelling my wish through my hands, into the metal and out its prongs across the ocean to find my daughter.

The galleon continues, leaving the safety of the coast, slicing fast through the waves with a budding wind that blasts through its sails like I want to blast Lea with this weapon's power. She appears on deck and crosses to its railings, still crying. She has to know she's not alone. She has to see me. She has to hear me.

So I surface quickly above the waves, hold out the trident again and scream her name. "Lea! Lea!" My words disappear into the groan of a whale, so deep and sonorous it sounds exactly how I feel.

But it makes no difference. Lea doesn't understand, the trident doesn't work, the galleon crosses into deep waters, and a coolness curls around my shoulders, making me shiver. A darkness descends. Scales on my tail prickle. And a periwinkle tint burgeons in the water, more vivid than ever before.

Merfolk are never to be seen. Yet Triton himself surfaces above the ocean, drawn in his silver and pearl chariot by two dolphins, and he races head-on towards the prince's galleon. With one hand gripping the reins, he raises his other hand, plucks a lightning bolt from the cloudless sky, and hurls it into the galleon's hull.

Wood detonates into splinters. Shards fling out. Water rushes in.

He flings another bolt, and another, until the galleon is perforated with holes. He booms something across the air, but his words are as formless as thunder, and sink as he does under the water once more.

The galleon sinks too, and Lea with it. Lea who is human now, with human legs and human lungs. She'll drown!

I dive down and immediately hear Triton's boom. "I will sink them all!" He circles the galleon in his chariot, enclosing it in a dark whirlpool that pulls it under.

"Lea!" I whimper, until the sound of it hardens into resolve. My daughter will not drown. I drive my body through the coursing water ahead. It dims and rushes and flings me aside. Still I push through to the whirlpool's ribbed surges, spiralling and twisting from the air in it. How do I get through? "Lea!"

Triton stops his dolphins and searches for my voice. Through the still-swirling water, he sees me and points. "How dare you even hold it! Return it to me!"

But the galleon is falling fast now, and in its drag bodies float as plentiful as sprouts in a seagrass meadow. Long rosy hair flows among them. A blue dress clings to useless legs. Arms claw for the surface. The trident could save her.

I grip it and swim down, though the galleon is already hitting the sea floor. Its hull crumbles into itself. Its bow cracks apart. Silt blooms up from its impact, swelling around Lea as she's pulled down with it. She closes her eyes, giving up. There's nothing more she can do, and my motionless daughter disappears among the sand's billowing powder. I dive anyway and find a hand. Her hand. Smooth and precious. I pull her to me and hold her close. I have her. I have the trident. But what now? I still don't know how the trident works.

"Seyla!" Triton bellows, leaving his chariot to plough towards us, his thrust so wrathful he pushes a rushing bank of water before him.

It blasts into me, as his wake usually does, spiralling me into the wreck, spiralling Lea with me too. We spin among the sand blooms, twisting out of control, until we thud into the galleon itself, through its quarterdeck and into a sunken cabin beneath.

A sharp pain sears through my tail. I scream out, flailing against whatever I'm impaled upon. It hurts like fire, like lava!

I reach to pull myself free… except no splintered plank or shard penetrates my tail – it's the trident itself, spearing me with an outer prong, hooking me with its teethed tip.

Blood rushes, gushing out of me. So much it cloaks me in a red cloud, drifts through the cracked holes above us. But I'm still alive, and my daughter needs me.

I yank the trident out, teethed tip and all, and the cloud of blood darkens.

But it's too late. Lea floats beside me. Motionless. Eyes closed. Drowned.

My tears stream, though they only help to clear my eyes so I can see… Lea's legs are melting together, their supple skin darkening to sea green. Scales form, more and more as her skin absorbs my blood. My blood is transforming her!

I curl my tail around her and squeeze, though it hurts like childbirth. I squeeze and squeeze until she opens her eyes, sees me. Alive.

A cool current swirls into the cabin – Triton coming to claim what's his. But Lea and I are no longer his. I put a finger to her mouth, then toss his trident up through my blood, propelling it through the hole in the cabin's ceiling. We move back into the shadows and wait.

He can think what he wants. He saw Lea drown. He can see my blood. If I were alive, I'd surely be sobbing in grief, screaming that he's to blame. My silence surely stones my grave.

He's silent himself a moment, accepting it, then a rushing whirl of water blasts into the cabin – him swimming away.

"How did you know," Lea asks after a while, "how to turn me back?"

"I didn't." I check my tail. The bleeding is slowing. "If our first king used his own blood to turn humans into merfolk, I've never heard of it. Have you?"

She shakes her head, her beautiful coral hair shimmering in the sunbeams now rotating through the settling aqua. I take her hand and peek through the holes we made, checking for Triton before swimming out and through a forest of drowned sailors.

Lea searches sadly among them. Probably looking for her prince. "Are they in heaven now?"

"Supposedly. Do you wish you were too?" I ask her honestly. "You might have found him there?"

Lea laughs. "I wouldn't want to meet that sea cucumber again. He had no spine! He didn't even know the girl he married, just did it because his father told him. That's when I realised, if I ever made it back to the sea, I would *never* live in the city again. There is a better way to die than never living."

I give her arm a squeeze. She's alive. Her *and* her vibrant mind.

"And those sailors," she gestures at them as we swim away, "I heard them speak of merfolk. They've seen them other places, in other seas."

"Then maybe we should go find them, together."

"What about your research?" Lea asks, surprised. "If we go back to your hollow, someone might see us."

I stop her and look into her eyes. "If the price of a soul is turning into a human, and that's the way humans treat a creature as kind and beautiful as my daughter…" I glance down at the faint trail of blood weeping out of me, and smile. "Then the only thing I'm concerned about now is my tail."

ABOUT 'A BLOODIED TAIL'

The archetype I wanted to explore was the vilified ex-partner, turned into evil incarnate by a vindictive spouse. In the original story of 'The Little Mermaid' by Hans Christian Andersen (1837), the mermaid's father is a sea king who "had been a widower for many years", but there is no explanation about how, when or why his wife died. There's also a sea witch who, although fearsome, lives nearby, and who the little mermaid hopes "can give me counsel and help". So I started to wonder, what if these two women were one and the same? What if the sea witch wasn't as evil as the sea king might want us to believe? What would have been his reasons for doing so, and what would be the result...

ABOUT ZENA SHAPTER

Zena Shapter writes from a castle in a flying city hidden by a thundercloud. Author of *When Dark Roots Hunt* (2023), *Towards White* (2017) and co-author of *Into Tordon* (2016), among others, she's won over a dozen writing competitions – including a Ditmar Award, Glen Miles Short Story Prize, and Australasian Horror Writers' Association Award for Short Fiction. Her short stories have appeared in many anthologies and magazines all around the world, including the Hugo-nominated Sci Phi Journal, Midnight Echo and their Australian Shadows Awarded 'best' anthology, Antipodean SF, and Award-Winning Australian Writing (twice). When not writing, Zena loves movies, frogs, chocolate, potatoes and living with her family among Sydney's beautiful Northern Beaches. She's travelled all around the world, visiting close to 50 countries, which inspire her to create worlds of her own. With her BA (Hons) in English Literature, Zena enjoys working as a mentor, editor and inclusive creativity advocate, inspiring writers to develop their craft. She teaches storytelling and writing at festivals, libraries and schools, judges various literary awards and encourages everyone to value the importance of creativity. She believes that stories are our best invention. Find her online via social media @ZenaShapter and zenashapter.com

CURSE OF THE FINEST

―――cᴧᴐ―――

MANDY MUNRO

Being the most desired man in all of Terrarealis took hard work and dedication. Edstern faced the digital integrate screen that comprised the wall of the master bedroom in his seven-level uptown penthouse known as the Palacé. The screen delivered an almost perfect reflection of Edstern. Almost perfect, except for the glitch in the code that created a single line of pixels across the centre of the screen.

Edstern rubbed the smooth skin around his eyes. No wrinkles. He smiled on the inside. An actual smile hadn't crossed his face in years. Beauty wasn't for the weak-willed, but… he snorted and adjusted his silk shirt over his waxed and well-formed pectoral muscles. The twenty-something-year-old that he'd employed that morning to manage his daily schedule, Prya was her name, hadn't spared him anything other than a cursory glance. What was her problem? *This* was beauty, not Porcelain, his nineteen-year-old stepson.

Edstern huffed and interlocked the fingers of his hands,

swivelled them in a downward motion and cracked them all at once. The highborn elites knew he was serious when he did that. Some even got on their knees and crawled into hiding in case he let loose one of his infamous digital curses – a quick loosening of his fingers across the nearest soft-touch screen and he could create a blinding code to block any nuisance's access to that day's episode of *I'm a Goldlink Mastercoder*. And if he was particularly peeved, he would lock them out of the weekly soirée he held at his Palacé, where the most advanced master codes were revealed. Being a spell crafter, born of the ancient race of Digi-mages, had its advantages.

Edstern composed himself, then danced his fingers over the spell-glitched integrate screen, entering the passcode phrase that opened the link to communicate with his twin sister in the ethavirtualis. "Gilly. Is there a woman who thinks I'm the finest in Terrarealis?" he typed.

His sister's face, framed by a mane of blonde hair, materialised in the massive screen. It was the only window into the virtual world, where she'd become trapped when their blasted digi-spell had backfired. Even with the orange night-mask across her eyes, she looked perfect – olive skin, high cheekbones, and full pouty lips. Not one hint of middle-age sag.

Edstern lifted his chin and smoothed the skin on his neck, which just so happened to be where the pixel line crossed the screen. Trying to digitally encode their beauty into their living bodies had been a brilliant idea when they were twenty-one and at their peak. They would've been proclaimed the finest twins in all of Terrarealis and lived forever. But the digi-spell had rebounded, which meant that while Gilly luxuriated in ageless beauty, he was stuck in Terrarealis with the task of breaking the digi-spell code so he could free her. It wasn't fair.

"Wait," Gilly cried, pulling the sleep mask from her eyes. "I wasn't ready, so the question doesn't count."

Edstern inhaled snootily and began speaking now that the ethavirtualis link was open. "Is there a woman–"

Gilly groaned and flounced her hair in silky waves over her shoulders. "Must we really have this conversation every day, Ed? You know I'm the finest twin, *and* I get to smile, and frown, and do this." She pressed her hands on both cheeks, making a fish face.

The digital sophistication of the integrate screen was so advanced, it looked like the real Gilly was right in front of him. Edstern almost reached out to poke her face. "Well, if I don't say or type in the question each day, Ms Eternally Beautiful," he snapped, "I will instantly age and die. And if you don't give me an answer that is true to me – same instant old-age-death-thing! So who got the worse end of the digi-spell?" He tugged a golden clip from his hair and let his blond locks infused with nanobots – a four-hundred-diyen-a-month, perfectly justifiable expense in his view – tumble over his shoulders. "Anyway, we're still a matching pair, except my hair glistens, for real."

"Just like your nose," Gilly giggled. "Anyway, real is overrated. It isn't so bad in here."

Edstern gritted his teeth, resisting the urge to throw something at the screen. He was a slave to the screen, until just one woman thought him to be the finest in Terrarealis – at which point the line across the screen would finally disappear, completing the code and breaking the digi-spell so Gilly could return to reality.

One woman. How hard could that be? He wouldn't have minded if it was a man, but it had to be a woman. Eighteen years had already passed, and he could only hold back aging for so long.

Edstern tapped the metal toe of his boot – the sound always got people's attention. "Listen to me, Gilly, I can't keep doing this every day, and I want my sister back." He was tired of being taunted with her eternal youth, and he wanted her out of the mirror, so they could hang out somewhere other than the Palacé like they used to. "So, I was reading about fuzzy logic the other day and I thought it might work with the digi-spell code."

"How's that?" Gilly lifted an eyebrow.

"Well, if we play with the digi-spell word and replace *finest* with a similar word – one that any woman or man might think of me – close enough might be good enough to bamboozle the code's logic. Here, I'll ask the question again." Edstern rubbed his hands together and quickly typed across the screen. "Is there a woman who thinks I'm the finest in Terrarealis?"

"The finest? Hmm…" Gilly stared up towards some imaginary sky and rubbed her chin thoughtfully. Exactly where she was in the ethavirtualis was a mystery to Edstern. Gilly lowered her eyes to stare at him. "Sorry, Ed. All women still think Porcelain is the finest. He was voted the Best Natural Body in this month's issue of *Terrarealis' Finest,* with special mention to his skin being so pale it could reflect digi-spells."

"That's a pile of bollocks," Edstern muttered. "He's as natural as the vat-load of nano-muscle-gel infused-with-bleach he gets delivered weekly to the Palacé. Whereas my body is crafted by hours in the gym and spending a fortune on self-care. How am I not the finest?"

"The consensus says otherwise," Gilly retorted.

"Yeah, yeah. Let's try another word," Edstern grumbled. He hated Porcelain, and it seemed worse that he was his stepson. "Is there a woman who thinks I'm the most *gorgeous* in Terrarealis?" he typed, then pressed the flat part of his finger to his forehead so the skin between his eyes didn't pucker.

His sister walked the length of the screen like it was a catwalk, turned at the end with her arms folded and pouted. She wore a purple lycra jumpsuit and was truly spectacular. "Now you're making it hard for me to answer true, Ed. Do you mean in the dazzling, magnificent way that made the girl you dated last week do all those acrobatic moves to impress you? The screen doesn't accept the thoughts of deluded women. Or do you mean in the boy-next-door fresh-as-a-daisy, melt-the-knees kind of way, like Porcelain? He has a cute little kitten that sits on his shoulder and goes with him everywhere, you know?"

Edstern wanted to drown that irritating feline and make it into a fur hat! He tore at his hair, then whipped his fingers across the screen. He had one last alternative word to try. "Is there a woman who thinks I'm the most *beautiful* in Terrarealis?"

"Beautiful?" Gilly's eyes widened as she strutted back to stand in front of him. "Beauty is in the eyes of the beholder! What one sees is all that matters. So, yes, it is you, brother! You are the most beautiful in Terrarealis and the code will break if…"

Edstern leapt up, flicked his fingers over the environ controls, and plunged his room into the luscious greens of the fair isles, complete with a blast of joyful pipe music. He danced on his toes with his arms straight at his side; it was a cute jig that always drew applause. "I am the most beautiful!" he sang, delighted that his sister agreed, even if Prya hadn't given him a glance. She was probably gay.

"If…" Gilly said loudly.

Edstern stopped dancing. He tapped the environ controls, returning the room to normality, and stared at Gilly.

"It will break if Porcelain is dead," Gilly said wincing. "You see, Prya – yes, I know about her too – does like you, but she can't get the boy out of her mind. When Porcelain is gone, lover-girl will agree that you are the most beautiful in Terrarealis, and she will only have eyes for you."

"Not fair!" Edstern yelled. "I'll get my chief digital scientist to swap Porcelain's entry card to the Palacé with an entry card to Club Blue Light, where he and his kitty can dance forever. No one *ever* comes out of there."

"I wouldn't advise you to do that, brother. The Club was coded by an ancient Digi-mage who also wanted to live forever young. Some say it uploads people to the ethavirtualis."

"As long as Porcelain's no longer here, that's fine with me." Edstern interlocked his fingers and cracked them viciously.

"Success tastes so sweet." Edstern sighed to himself and tossed back what was left of his cocktail. He placed the empty glass on the shelf and turned to smile at his reflection in the integrate screen. He spun Porcelain's embossed Palacé entry card on its fine golden chain in the air, and studied thin line of pixels across the screen. They seemed fainter than yesterday.

"Gilly," he typed. "Is there a woman who thinks I'm the finest in Terrarealis?"

"You know the answer. I'm tired. Go away." The words appeared in white CAPS across the screen.

Edstern stamped his foot and typed. "Nonsense! Hurry up. I've asked the question."

Gilly's face emerged as the pixels tuned to render her perfect ageless beauty. A frilly yellow sleep mask covered her eyes, and she yawned something unintelligible. Her shoulders were bare. Edstern's mouth dropped. "Are you naked?"

A coy smile appeared on Gilly's face as she pulled off her mask. "I might have had a friend stay."

"G-G, I'm waiting," a woman cooed from somewhere Edstern couldn't see.

Oh. He flushed hot. Even his sister in the ethavirtualis could get some and he... Edstern quickly glanced inside his silk shirt at the pectoral muscles he worked so hard to keep firm and looking like they belonged to someone twenty years younger. Of course he was sexy.

"I don't care what your behind-the-screen activities are," Edstern sniffed, and spun the entry card vigorously. The chief digital scientist – a well-built man with muscled arms, hair on his chest and a tight toosh – had promised to have a cocktail with him later today. Not all Edstern's dates had be with women.

Gilly smirked. "You do care. I have fun in here."

Another taunt. Did she really have to appear so happy in her perfect virtual world? "Well, Porcelain is gone now," he huffed, "and soon you will be joining me in Terrarealis."

Gilly raised an eyebrow, then leaned over the edge of the screen, staring at the embossed card in his hand.

Edstern had to look away – his sister's breasts looked perkier than his pecs. The screen must have warped.

"Is that what I think it is?" Gilly asked.

"Yes!" Edstern almost smiled.

His sister straightened, so only her cleavage showed. "Well, it's not what you think it is."

"What?"

A sound came out of Gilly that could easily have been mistaken for a pig squealing. She put a hand to her mouth and the other across her breasts to stop them jiggling. "That card isn't for the Palacé, it's for the boudoir where I kept my handcuffs and collar. I used to give them to my lovers before I got stuck in here." She glanced at the pixelated line across the screen and shrugged.

"I hate to break it to you, Ed, but Porcelain still lives and is the finest."

"No!" Edstern wailed. "That beastly chief scientist *lied* to me. He told me I was so handsome he struggled to breathe when I was near him!"

Gilly's expression softened. "You weren't to know, brother. I see the truth. I'm also the most intelligent of us, but that's beside the point."

"What *is* your point?" Edstern fumed, snapping the card in two and throwing the pieces on the floor. His vacuum shot out from the wall, sucked the fragments into its belly with a slurping sound, and zoomed back to its dock.

"The point is you need to get rid of Porcelain yourself. I can help."

Edstern stared at her. "The last time you helped involved *me* eating several buckets of berries and spending three days on the toilet."

Gilly's eyes widened innocently. "Unfortunate, I admit." She tapped the edge of the screen with a flurry of finger movements – she too was a spell crafter. She smiled encouragingly. "Come on. Let's see where Porcelain is and make a plan."

Edstern snorted rudely and folded his arms. "No matter what you suggest, I won't do anything I don't want to."

"Of course," Gilly said, and stepped out of sight. The integrate screen changed to display a single-story duplex with gravel-rolled painted walls and shuttered windows. There were equally dilapidated duplexes on either side and more of the same opposite. The uptown Skytower was a beacon of hope in the distance, with its constantly flickering screens showing news and success in equal measure.

"The salubrious bowels of downtown Terrarealis…" Edstern began to say, then faltered.

A slender young man with pale skin and tousled brown hair was spray-painting a brightly coloured mural onto the wall of the duplex. There was something captivating about his fragile appearance, as though he might break somehow. The mural was reminiscent of post-modernist art, when modernism was a thing – eons ago. The fluffy ginger and white kitten balanced on the man's shoulder occasionally swiped its paw at the can of paint. Edstern scowled. His stepson's preference for creating retro art with a can of paint – instead of mastering digital virtuosity where art was only limited by your digi-spells and the dexterity of your fingers over the screen – made him a disgrace to their family of Digi-mages.

"Porcelain must have a headache with that kitty constantly meowing in his ear," Gilly commented.

"Shush, I'm watching!" Edstern snapped.

Jesperi, one of the Shaw women who ran a natural gym in the collaborator district, was flying up the street on a decades-old magna board powered by nano-sparks, which meant it only hovered an inch above the ground. The Magna Mark-11 that Edstern had invented, ran on nano-explosions, and could fly anywhere.

Jesperi was a pretty thing in her early thirties with spiked black hair, and a fondness for wearing tops with whales printed on them, tartan minis, and laced-up boots. Edstern had tried to ask Jesperi out once. The nano-infused switch-blade she carried was very, very sharp.

Porcelain turned and waved as Jesperi swung into the front yard and hopped off the magna board. The knot of jealousy in Edstern's stomach tightened. The sneaky boy had an older woman.

Wait! Nicky and Paula also walked into the duplex's front yard from the street. Nicky was the twenty-something-year-old who worked in the fire-bean café not far from the Palacé and knew Edstern's daily drink order. Her mop of rusty coloured hair, deep voice, broad shoulders, and legs well-rounded from hours of doing squats, had always piqued Edstern's interest.

And Paula, easily recognisable by her permanent glassy-eyed gaze from smoking too many vega-leaves – the digi-spelled tree was a favourite of creatives who used to it enhance their imagination. And was that… Mica? Porcelain's best friend had come out of the duplex in paint-spattered overalls, holding another can of paint. Mica had treated his hair with nanobots, so it constantly changed colour, and he had a nose ring.

Edstern felt his blood rise. Porcelain had formed a commune!

"The second lass with the firm buttocks reminds me of you, brother."

"And Glassy-eyes could be you, Gilly. You and your vices."

"Don't throw stones, Ed. Everyone's got at least one." Gilly's tone was knowing. "I've seen you–"

"Are you watching?" Edstern yelled, pointing at the screen. "Look!"

Porcelain kissed each woman as they passed into the duplex, and – Edstern blinked – Porcelain kissed Mica passionately too.

"You've raised quite the man-about-the-town," Gilly's tone was admiring.

"How can my nineteen-year-old stepson have three women and a boy wrapped around his finger?" Edstern shouted. All he wanted was just one person in his life. A woman or a man – he wouldn't be choosy. Curse the boy! Edstern quickly pressed between his forehead and smoothed out the scowl lines.

"Just saying, everyone likes smiles and kisses, and even the odd wrinkle and fat-roll to squeeze, if that's where your fancy lies," Gilly said.

"My wife didn't," Edstern muttered. He'd strived so hard to be the finest in everything for her, and had created the most amazing digi-spells environs to please her, but to no avail. So after seventeen years of marriage, he'd secretly killed his darling wife because, while he had loved her, Porcelain's fragile beauty kept reminding her of her first husband, so even she could not break the digi-spell for Edstern.

Edstern exhaled bitterly. Jesperi stroked Porcelain's hair. Glassy-eyed Paula held Porcelain's hands, while Nicky presented him with a fire-bean drink. Now Mica was pushing all the women out of the way and kissing Porcelain again.

Edstern shut his eyes. Porcelain had everything he didn't.

"He's going to be busy for a while, brother. Young and fair

trumps maturity at its finest. How's it going with that young Prya you like?"

Edstern paced the floor in front of the screen. "I'm going to kill Porcelain, then every woman and man will worship at my feet!" Edstern was suddenly quite breathless. His gym regime didn't include cardio.

His sister bit off a fingernail, then flicked it away. "Fine. Since I'm the brains in the family, Edstern, this is what we're going to do."

Edstern's neck, shoulders, buttocks, and legs were unnaturally clenched as he flew his Magna Mark-11 slowly along the dark and exceedingly narrow downtown streets. Balancing used to be a breeze, but the digi-spelled master code he'd used to create his disguise added thirty years to his age, and staying upright on a moving plank as a seventy-year-old was almost impossible. His atrophying bones ached horrendously. Not only that, but his eyesight was blurred even with the control glasses he wore, and it terrified him that he might run into something in the gloom of night. Gilly had promised the aging digi-spell would only work on the outside, but it didn't feel that way.

"Edstern!" her muffled electronic voice called from inside his long coat.

Edstern blinked at the vision-controlled speed dial on the inside of his glasses. A droplet of water ran down his cheek, and miraculously his eyesight cleared. It seemed that overactive tear ducts were the cause of his vision loss. He blinked and brought the Mack-11 to a stop on the pavement next to a garbage bin. His nose and mouth screwed up with distaste – old age hadn't dampened his olfactory senses.

He tugged the portable integrate screen from his coat pocket and held it up, his wrinkled hand quivering with the effort. He almost screamed at the device's interpretive reflection of his face. His skin was wizened with creases (not including the line of cursed pixels across the display). He'd grown a rusty orange beard, and his earlobes had lengthened the same way his grandfetter's had!

"He he," Gilly chuckled out of the device in a digitally generated voice. "What does it feel like, letting yourself go?"

"I hate your plan!" Edstern croaked, tapping his fingers across the screen so he could see her. Turning himself into a hideous old man wasn't the scheme he'd imagined, but Gilly had insisted it was the only way. He suspected it had something to do with the amusement of seeing him aged.

Gilly's perfect face appeared in the mirror.

"What do you want?" Edstern snapped.

"Do you have the can of spray paint?"

"Yes." Edstern checked his other coat pocket to be sure.

"Do you know the escape route?"

"Of course." He tapped his glasses and called up a map of the downtown streets. "Follow Bong Bong Street to the central square, but don't go up the Party-to-death strip that runs parallel to it." It led to Club Blue Light.

"Do you have spare undies?"

Edstern reached for his chest pocket, then stopped indignantly. "What's that got to do with anything?"

Gilly chewed her red lip. "You were clenching so tight back there and old men aren't known for their bodily control."

"Gilly!" Edstern cried indignantly.

"It's true!" His sister grinned, then her smile disappeared. "Now, get going. You'll have to walk and take the fork in the path just ahead. Your art competition is about to start."

His art competition – where he'd destroy his stepson in a spray paint contest. With Gilly's help he'd infused his mage skin with a digi-spell enabling him to impersonate Van God, one of the greatest artists of all time. Bring it on, Porcelain. Let's see who really is the finest!

Edstern stashed the Mack-11 behind the bin and began shuffling up the narrow street. Had Gilly said to take the left or right fork? A doof, doof sound tugged him to the left. There were red lights over doors, odd noises he couldn't quite place but that might have been his old-age hearing, and a sweet tang in the air that made him feel nauseous. The blue glow at the end of the street seemed like a target – it must be where the art competition was being held. Edstern shuffled with purpose. He and Gilly had run through several different plans but this one seemed inspired, killing Porcelain while he was doing something he loved.

Something banged Edstern's shoulder, sending him stumbling

onto his knees. His glasses slid from his nose. He groaned but at least he hadn't faceplanted.

Hands grabbed him beneath the shoulders, lifting him roughly. He felt so disoriented. Where was his strength? He struggled pathetically.

"Hey, old dude. You should be in bed, not on the streets this late."

Edstern blinked into a couple of blurry faces; at least one was a boy from the deep tone. Hands brushed over Edstern, and he felt fingers slide into the pocket over his chest. He grabbed the wrist as the hand pulled out his spare undies.

"I need those," Edstern growled.

"You old creep!" the boy shrieked, struggling to free himself.

"Come on, Enzo," a girl shouted. "The competition's about to begin."

Edstern was only too happy for them to run away, but now he was as good as blind. His tear ducts really did have a mind of their own and he had no hope of finding his glasses. He shoved his hand in his coat pocket, and was relieved to grasp the portable integrate device. He moved his trembling fingers over the screen and held it up.

"Gilly, I need you to guide me," his voice quavered.

"Edstern?" Gilly's monotone answer held no urgency. "What have you done?"

Edstern wiped his eyes. Maybe some of the water was actual tears. He sniffed. "I was attacked and lost my glasses. I need you to tell me where to go. I can hear the crowd up ahead."

"Chin up, brother," Gilly said flatly. "Hold the screen higher and turn on the spot so I can look around."

Edstern did as he was told.

"You're wobbling so bad you're making me sick. You're in a narrow alley... blast it, Ed, you're in the Party-to-death strip, but wait... Porcelain's coming this way instead of going to the competition. He's got his kitty on his shoulder, but that shouldn't be a bother. Quick! There's a blank wall on your left. You don't need the competition. Just stick with the plan."

Edstern shoved the portable screen into one pocket and pulled out the can of spray paint. He fumbled with the lid, shuffled to the wall, pressed down the nozzle and began to paint. He let a film of coloured droplets fall onto his hand. The nanobots entered his skin, activating the digi-spell he'd cast on himself before leaving home. A carefree feeling came over him and he found himself muttering as he sprayed. "Green is for grass. Gold is for hay. Purple is for skies and the midnight blues."

"Van God?" Porcelain exclaimed. "I can't believe I'd find you painting in the streets of downtown! I'd recognise your golden wheatfields anywhere. When I heard that the digi-reincarnation codes had brought you back, all I've dreamed is meeting you."

There was such wonder in Porcelain's voice, a small part of Edstern was pleased he'd fulfilled his stepson's greatest dream before killing him; but he kept painting with wide strokes of his spray can. The digi-spell moving through his body made the motion of painting mesmerising – even if he couldn't see what he was doing.

"I gather you aren't competing at the Natural Creator's Competition. May I join you instead?" Porcelain asked in a hopeful tone.

Edstern turned and smiled through his watery eyes at the fuzzy human shape that was Porcelain. The orange and white purring blob on his stepson's shoulder looked like it had a strange second head. One or both of those heads needed to die.

The kitty stood on all fours and hissed. It had never liked Edstern. "Stop it, Topaz," Porcelain scolded.

Edstern held out his spray can. "It would be my pleasure," he said and squirted paint over both Porcelain and the kitty.

Porcelain screamed and Topaz jumped to the ground. But the nanobots in the paint were already creating their own art – the code in them sought out weakness in surfaces, so were burrowing into Porcelain's skin, already paper thin from the bleach in the muscle-gel he used to make his body buff. Now his pale skin was disintegrating.

Suddenly, Edstern was glad his eyesight was so bad. He backed away from where Porcelain writhed on the ground, whimpering. Edstern couldn't be certain, but he thought Porcelain murmured "Kill the bastard, Topaz," before dying on the street.

Edstern stood there a moment. Killing Porcelain hadn't given him the satisfaction he thought it might. He also had a massive pain on the left side of his chest and down his arm. It felt like his heart was giving out. He pulled out the portable integrate screen from his pocket, blinking back tears so he could peer at the display while running his fingers over it to call Gilly.

"Did you kill him, Ed?" Gilly's electronic voice was excruciatingly slow compared to Edstern's painfully racing heart.

Edstern also felt very hot, and the air moved as though someone had turned on one of the enormous warm fans that heated downtown during winter. "I did, sister." Edstern held up the screen so she could see.

"Argh!" It took a moment for Edstern to realise the long, drawn-out sound was Gilly screaming in monotone. Screaming at what?

A hiss came from above him.

Edstern looked up into the bared teeth of a yellow, green, and blue cat. He didn't need glasses to see it – Topaz had grown enormous. "The nanobots," he muttered, remembering an article he'd read last year, about how certain animals were allergic to nanobots, which caused their cells to multiply, creating gigantors like Topaz. "Kitty must have been allergic."

"Run!" Gilly said.

Edstern tottered up the alley. The pain in his heart was really bad, but he made it to the pulsating door of Club Blue Light. The enormous kitten bounded towards him. The Club was the only exit from the alley, but this was the place where people went in and never came out, like his sister in the ethavirtualis…

His heart stuttered painfully – soon he would die and… A thought smacked him in the head. He pulled out the screen and this time pressed dictate. "Gilly!" he cried. "Who's the finest in Terrarealis?" His words splayed in white text across the screen.

Gilly's voice crackled with static, her answer was a garbled mess of monotone notes.

But as Topaz raised its paw to swipe, Edstern gripped his chest in pain, and fell through the door.

Edstern opened his eyes. He lay in a four-poster bed made with satin sheets and plump pillows. The scent of roses wafted in the air, and an elaborate bath on golden feet occupied the corner of the plush room. If this was death, it didn't look so bad.

He rolled over and saw a full-length mirror attached to the wall. A mirror? They'd been relegated to museums eons ago. He blinked at an attractive middle-aged man wearing silk pyjamas, lying in bed.

Horror filled him as he slowly raised his hand to his grey hair. It was *him* in the mirror!

Edstern scrambled out of bed and gaped at his reflection. He pressed at the pair of wrinkles between his eyes, raised his chin and smoothed the fall of soft skin on his neck. He actually didn't look that bad, natural. He shuddered. It was better than spending eternity as a hideous old man, but still... he was old. He turned and admired the drape of the silk shirt falling over his pectorals – still firm, even in death.

"Just saying, your right pec is more developed than your left."

"Gilly!" Edstern spun, clasping his chest.

His middle-aged twin sister was perched on the bed in a

slinky negligée, with a lovely dark-haired woman in a scandalous pair of pyjamas kneeling behind, massaging Gilly's shoulders. A gorgeous man in a kaftan stood next to them.

"Yes, it's me; and yes, you're in the ethavirtualis." Gilly smiled. "With Porcelain dead, you would have been the finest in Terrarealis, had you changed back into your old self in time. But, by entering the ethavirtualis of your own will – even though it was more Topaz swiping at you – you broke the curse! Well, part of the curse. The part about living forever. Not the youth bit." She held out her arms, admiring the wrinkles. "I may not be real, but I am my real age. I can get use this!" She grinned and hugged him tightly. "At least we're together now, Ed."

Edstern's eyes watered and he blinked as she let him go. His tear ducts were doing their thing again. He bit his tongue about Gilly having more wrinkles than him and made a show of straightening his pyjama shirt – he was with his sister at last. And, there was still the deliciously dark-haired man standing with Gilly. He was such a *manly* man, and he hadn't stopped looking at him.

"Did the cat get your tongue, Ed?" Gilly laughed. "This is Kamal. I think you'll like him. He was an evil sorcerer once banished by a genie to a magic lamp."

"Reformed sorcerer," Kamal declared, going down on one knee. He took Edstern's hand and kissed it. "You are the finest man in all the lands I have seen, and…" his black eyes twinkled wickedly, "I can show you my lamp, if you'd like?"

For the first time since Edstern could remember, he smiled.

ABOUT 'CURSE OF THE FINEST'

The bully archetype is often motivated by events in their past, and I wanted to explore a bully who, on the surface, appeared to have good reason to be a bully, though in fact was responding to something hidden to the world. The original story of 'Snow White' – a German fairy tale, first published in 'Grimm's Fairy Tales' (1812) by the Brothers Grimm – tells of an evil queen who possesses a magic mirror, which she asks every morning "Mirror mirror on the wall, who is the fairest one of all?" There has never been any explanation as to whom the person in the mirror was, and I began to wonder if perhaps they might be trapped in some way. Furthermore, the quest to be beautiful to satisfy vanity is what motivated the original evil queen, but what if the quest to be beautiful meant something else and wasn't about vanity at all?

ABOUT MANDY MUNRO

Mandy lives in the Northern Beaches of Sydney but has travelled extensively, gathering inspiration and research for her writing. The first book of Mandy's YA fantasy series was longlisted in the Page Turner 2022 Writing Awards, is a Finalist in the Page Turner 2023 Writing Awards. Her fantasy short story 'The Beastly Sound of Silence', is published in the fantasy e-zine *Tales of Netherün* (Vol 9, 2023) by Quill and Read. Mandy regularly beta-reads novels and is an active member of both the NBWG and a group of speculative fiction writers.

MR SMITH'S BAD DAY

MARK WHITE

Gloria was going to propose tonight, John just knew it. He'd seen her hiding something in the wardrobe, and when she was in the shower he'd found a box with the most beautiful engagement ring. Dear, sweet Gloria – to think of proposing even though he was between jobs. That's how much faith she had in him.

"Wear that nice suit of yours, John," she'd told him before she left for work. "We're going to the restaurant where we had our first date."

First, though, he and his nice suit had to get through the day. He'd have to be careful not to spill anything on it, though wearing a suit would at least come in useful for his meeting at the hospital – his mum had always told him to look smart when meeting important people.

He drove into the hospital car park and immediately saw a man get into his vehicle. He approached to take the space, then waited. John drummed his fingers on the steering wheel and muttered curses to himself, glancing at his wrist as the seconds-hand of his watch swept on. How long had he been here already? Fifteen minutes? Yes, he would be late for his appointment now. What was taking the man so long?

He peered closer at the driver. The man was on his phone, chatting away and admiring his reflection in the rear-view mirror. John knew his type. They'd made his life an endless misery at school. Tall, handsome, and sporty; not John, not with his limp hair and weak knees.

In a different world he'd get out of his car, march over and knock on the window and say, "Hey, buddy, some of us have got a life to live, so scram!" Mr Tall and Handsome would swallow and say, "Yes, sir, right away," put the phone down and reverse out of the space as if his life depended on it… because he knew his challenger was capable of anyth–

Screeeeeech.

John refocused on the world to see a ute claim his space, Mr Tall and Handsome nowhere in sight.

"Damn it!" he muttered.

It took him another half an hour to find a park on the street, and only then by recklessly doing to someone else what had just been done to him. Luckily, his opponent this time was an old woman. Even then, she'd turned the air blue with all her cursing.

As if she had indeed cursed him, the heavens opened just as he hurried along the street, first a little and then all the way. He opened his trusty umbrella, but something tiny pinged off one of the struts and struck his face, causing a sudden sting as the whole thing collapsed. He pulled it from his face and warily patted his cheek, staring at the slick of blood that the increasingly torrential rain then washed off his hand in seconds.

John flexed his arms and tilted his head up. Water hammered on his face. He drew in a breath to scream 'Why?', only the downpour hit his back of his throat, making him cough and splutter.

"Here, mister," a small voice said. He opened his eyes to see a little girl, maybe five or six years old, looking at him with a solemn expression. She held out a tiny pink umbrella emblazoned with a unicorn jumping over a rainbow. "I want you to have this."

John was ninety minutes late by the time he arrived at the clinic, which was hidden away in a distant annexe of the hospital along endless identical corridors, all painted the same bilious green. The heating was too high, making him sweat. He burst through the doors, his breath hitching in his throat, his heart hammering, and faced the receptionist, who was staring at a screen. She was sixty if she was a day, but still fearsome.

"I-I-I-I," he stammered.

She held up a finger while remaining fixated on the screen.

He dropped the little girl's pink umbrella, which hit the floor with a plop.

The noise attracted the gorgon's attention and she looked up, her lip curling slightly. "Name?" she asked, her voice also curling up slightly.

"Mr John Smith." His voice cracked as his breath slowed.

She tutted. "We'd given up on you. Do you know how late you are? Mr Cheswell's a very busy man. His next patient's just gone in – they could be an hour, easily."

John's head began to throb, shame dumping all manner of hormones into his body. His mouth felt sour, little pricks of tears formed in his eyes, and he felt as if he'd never be dry again.

The sound of water trickling onto the linoleum floor from his left sleeve broke the silence. The gorgon tutted a second time. "Change into this and I'll get those *things* dried." She fished around under her desk, retrieving a blue hospital gown.

The gesture of kindness was so unexpected that he burst into tears. "Th-thank you," he stammered again. "I'm having a bad day."

A tut and a grimace. "Oh, it's not for you. Mr Cheswell's had new carpet fitted. If I let you go in there and drip everywhere, I'll never hear the end of it."

John took the gown and went into the toilets to change.

"Well, come in, man. Better late than never!"

John sighed with relief. He'd spent a sleepless week imagining the results of his annual screening: would the specialist look sad or worried or – worst of all – full of pity?

But Mr Cheswell wore a big smile – fitting for such a big man, with such outside bonhomie and giant hands, albeit accompanied with a raised eyebrow. "Take a seat. Mind when you do, though, – that suit looks a little tight. We don't want you to damage the crown jewels!"

John gave as big a chuckle as he dared, then closed the door behind him. His suit had come back dry, but had shrunk. The gorgon's expression dared him to say something, so he had just thanked her, went back to the toilets and squeezed himself into it. He could feel the pinch in his arms, legs and torso. What would Gloria say when she saw it? Would his inability to protect her favourite suit scare her off?

He walked across the thick, dark-blue carpet, his dry footsteps swallowed by the luxurious pile, and sat down as carefully as he could in the functional metal chair. The tearing sound from his groin was over in a brisk zip, and at least the pressure there lessened.

Mr Cheswell tilted his head down as he typed on his keyboard – he had fantastically thick black hair, which John coveted. "The results are in, I'm glad to say. Can you confirm your name and address?"

"John Smith, 33a Waratah Gardens, South Sydney."

Mr Cheswell's smile evaporated, as if it had never been there. "Can you repeat that, please?"

His throat went bone dry. "John Smith, 33a Waratah Gardens, South Sydney."

"Oh." Mr Cheswell stared at his computer display as if he'd found evidence of alien life. He started clicking away with his mouse.

John waited and waited, but all Mr Cheswell did was click his mouse. *Click click click click click.*

He then gave the longest and weariest sigh John had ever heard. "My dear fellow, I'm so sorry. Can you believe there are two John Smiths in the system?"

He trailed out of the hospital, walking randomly through the back streets towards his car. He dimly registered that it was raining – not heavily but persistently, and enough to make his shrunken suit damp, then wet again.

'Prognosis uncertain,' he thought, echoing Mr Cheswell's words.

At least he had Gloria.

The suit! No way he could turn up looking like this. But where could he…

A large black bird swooped past his head at speed. Surely it was too early in the season for magpies? John turned his head to see the bird ruffling its feathers across the street on the sign of a shop – a tailor's shop.

Could he? Gloria always liked to choose his clothes.

'A new leaf,' he thought. 'And you're about to have a fresh start as the future Mr Gloria.'

There was a headless tailor's dummy in the window with a measuring tape slung around its neck. In another window was a very fetching charcoal suit – almost a green-grey – that John fell instantly in love with. In such a suit he could do anything – defy an uncertain prognosis, impress at his very next job interview, dodge bullets, leap cars, apprehend villains, accept Gloria's proposal. "Yes," he murmured. "Yes, I will."

He checked, but there was no price tag attached. The window display was rather basic, given the finery on offer. Maybe it was a new shop? That didn't seem likely, though, given the frontage's dated appearance – dark wood, beams running along the top and bottom of the windows resolving to ornate spirals at the corners. Perhaps it had an old owner?

John pushed the door open, which jangled in welcome.

The shop looked empty. Subdued lighting left curious shadows.

"Hello," he called out, and the word was swallowed up in the silence.

The door jangled behind him again, making him jump. He turned to see the man from the hospital car park – Mr Tall and Handsome himself – enter the shop. He had black hair with a side parting and eyes that sparkled with health. He was also as dry as a bone, moving to the counter and striking a gold bell marked with the word 'Service'. A name plate next to it read: 'Proprietor Mr L Cypher'.

A droplet of rain ran down John's nose.

A moment later, a second man entered the room from somewhere. An alcove, probably, hidden from sight – not someone hunched and aged, but in his early 50s, brown hair not yet greying, fit-looking. "Mr Cavanaugh!" he cried. "Your suit is ready. It's perfect."

"*Lou*, my dude!" Mr Cavanaugh said, nodding, then flashing a smile. "Mr Cypher, you're the best in the business."

The smile made John hate Mr Cavanaugh even more. It spoke of effortlessly easing through the world, of people saying 'yes' and 'of course' and 'I don't usually, but in this case'.

"I hope you don't mind," Mr Cypher said, "but I've been displaying your suit in the window. It turned out so well I thought it might drum up some trade."

Mr Cavanaugh shook his head. "Share the love, my dude; share the love."

The proprietor turned to John, bowed – a formal gesture, almost taken from a history book – and handed him a towel, saying, "Apologies, sir, I'll be with you presently." Then he walked to the window and retrieved the beautiful charcoal suit, tearing John's heart asunder. The towel hung in his hand, its purpose forgotten. His eyes pricked again with tiny tears as Mr Cavanaugh examined the suit's seams and cut by holding it up to the odd mottled daylight. Then came that smile again.

Bastard.

John thought – felt, even – that the shop's proprietor *was* watching him, and when he glanced across, he was watching. The man's smile seemed ancient, like a mountain, though on reflection he couldn't be much older than thirty.

"Thanks, dude," said Mr Cavanaugh. "Usual terms?"

"Yes, Mr Cav-a-naugh," Mr Cypher said, splitting the name into syllables, his unblinking gaze still on John. "Usual terms."

The jingling of the doorbell told John that his nemesis had left the shop. Now the two of them were alone, and the silence held a different quality – it was as if the air itself was pressing upon them, eager to know their secrets. The room even seemed to spin slightly, giving him a sense of vertigo.

"You hate him," said Mr Cypher. The words were a simple statement.

"Yes," John said. "He parked in my spot, which wrecked my suit. And now he has my new suit. It's *my* suit!" he shouted. "*My* suit! *My* suit! *My* suit!"

He supposed he might have shouted forever if the kindly man had not clasped his shoulder. John wondered if the man was running a fever – his touch was so uncomfortably warm.

"You can get the suit," Mr Cypher told him slowly. "Mr Cavanaugh too, if you wish. But there's a price. A favour well done surely deserves a favour in return."

John squirmed out of the man's grip, but was unable to escape his gaze. His pupils had expanded to fill his eyes, all black now. It must be a trick of the light. Yes, it had to be the light, because now there was also a vertical slit in each eye, glowing a fiery orange. "I thought he was your friend?" John said.

"My friend?" Mr Cypher laughed. "I have no friends. I have clients, and anyone can be a client. They just have to ask – and agree to my terms."

John almost didn't dare ask, but Gloria was waiting – the

words he longed to hear poised to fall out of her beautiful mouth as she took to one knee. "The suit. Do you mean to say you have others in stock?"

The man – his eyes normal again – sized up John, and smiled. "I think I've got one in your size. What's it worth to you?"

"Anything," John said. "Anything for Gloria. The world and everything in it."

"Well, then," the man said, "it sounds as if we will indeed be operating on our usual terms."

"Do I need to sign for it?"

The man's eyes were black again. "Your word is enough. Your name?"

"John Smith."

"Welcome, Mr Smith." He unfurled his fist to reveal a pair of sunglasses with frames that reminded John of lozenges. "Please, try these on."

John took them and put them on. Instead of darker, his vision became as clear as he could remember.

"Great," Mr Cypher said. "They suit you, so to speak. And they'll help you watch people without them knowing – which I'll need you to do if you work for me. I'm looking to hire someone to assist me in security matters, some digital work. Are you available? You'll run across people like Mr Cav-a-naugh on a regular basis – and I'll wager him, too. We do tend to operate in the grey areas though, you should know that up front."

"Security?" John asked. "I don't know anything about security."

"It'll come naturally," Mr Cypher said, "if you trust me. *Officer Smith*, *do* you trust me?"

Officer Smith. John liked the sound of that. But he had one final question. "This new job, these favours you want in return, can it all wait until after dinner with Gloria?"

"Of course!" Mr Cypher said. "I have all the time in the world. More, for my best clients."

Smith smiled.

He put on his new suit, which was a perfect fit, then realised that his hair was a mess, so towelled it dry and smoothed it into place. He put on his sunglasses and admired himself in the changing room mirror. He sensed a new beginning starting that moment, a world in which he'd always get the parking space.

ABOUT 'MR SMITH'S BAD DAY'

Watching a number of futuristic thrillers and mafia movies recently (such as *The Matrix* and *The Godfather*), I noted how sharply dressed many fictional villains are in these genres. Usually it's because they have gained wealth from their various power plays, doing favours for others, operating in grey areas, motivated as they are by revenge and pride and high stakes. But what were those archetypal villains like before they became so? Weren't they just everyday men and women trying to get by? Imagine, if you will, a downtrodden man having a bad day when everything goes wrong, culminating in him needing a new suit. A strange tailor has the perfect fit in stock, although there's a price to pay, a favour to ask – agreeing to a grey area digital security job that also offers the chance of revenge. Would that be enough to change a person? It would all depend on the day…

ABOUT MARK WHITE

Mark White was born in the north of England and now counts himself very lucky to live a short amble from a beautiful Sydney beach. He grew up reading Ray Bradbury and later Philip K. Dick, and likes writing speculative fiction about how technology changes us. When not clattering away at a keyboard, he can be found exercising body and soul, and keeping the plants on his balcony green and healthy.

THE GREAT FISH

SUE OSBORNE

The gliding shark dreamed of her ancestral nursery, a place only known to her kind, where the currents were warm and there was a forest of long seaweed, whose tendrils would provide a haven for her young.

Her offspring squirmed in her belly, chasing and consuming weaker siblings in utero, practising their hunting skills, ready for ejection into the vast ocean. Their chances of survival were minimal, as they would likely be gobbled up by some other big fish soon after they were born. Only those ready to kill would be lucky enough to survive.

The mother had been swimming for days now, looking for shoals of fish along the shore to scoop into her great mouth. But she had found none. Every time she passed this coastline there were less and less fish. Instead, great shadowy beasts scooped up all the fish in giant billowing mouths before she even had a chance to hunt. As she passed under these mysterious shadows, her flanks vibrated, every sensor in her body shooting warning signals to her brain. These creatures reeked of blood. The terrified death throes of thousands of fish emanated from their hulking bodies. They looked like whales, but did not act like whales.

On their backs were the shadowy forms of other creatures, strange upright parasites that lived off them. She could not grasp what they were, or why they were there, but she did sense they were dangerous.

This evening, with the moon's reflection undulating on the waves, all was quiet, no strange giants were fishing nearby. She swam near the surface, enjoying the sensation of water rushing past her dorsal fin. She flicked her streamlined body from side to side. Water flowed through her nostrils, and she tried to detect any signs of fish in distress, or perhaps a seal mid-hunt. Along her flanks and around her head, tiny pores sensed changes in water pressure. She listened, she felt, she lived the water, ready for the tiniest message that might indicate a meal.

It had been weeks since her last feed and the desperate craving to eat, combined with the unrelenting pushing and banging on her insides, made her ready to take risks. If she didn't feed soon, she might die before she reached the nursery.

An uneven vibration made her turn, a strange rhythmic crashing against the surface of the water. She couldn't identify the creature making this noise, but with a contraction of her muscular body, she moved nearer to the source. A shudder of excitement rushed through her as she moved closer and began circling around and under the agitated water. The steady rhythm of the tide was broken by the weird thrashing of… what was it?

She sensed neither fish nor seal. There was an unnatural scent, something that didn't belong in her realm. She *had* to know what this was, and whether she could eat it.

She took a tentative bite, but it tasted awful. Blood from the creature swirled around her nostrils, and mouth, repulsing her. She spat it out, disappointed by the acidic taste. The pores along her body and head automatically closed to protect her from potential poison. With a quick flip of her tail, she turned away from the alien object.

When she glanced back, she thought she recognised the familiar outline of one of the parasites that lived on the large fishing beast. But it was motionless and clouded in too much blood for her to be certain.

She headed out to deeper ocean, soon smelling and tasting familiar fish blood in the water. Lots of it, floating near the surface. She torpedoed through the water towards it, her dorsal fin leaving a wake as she sped to the source of the blood before another of her kind could reach it. The scent was pungent, and sure to attract others.

Then she saw it, an injured fish, flopping about near the surface. She lined it up, lunged and grabbed it. As she bit down on the fish, though, something pierced her mouth. She shook her head violently, an excruciating pain ripping through her skull.

With her head above the water, she pulled away from the pain, but it did not stop.

That's when she saw it. One of the beasts was right next to

her. And its parasites were looking down at her. She was being dragged towards them.

She pulled back with all her might, but the thing kept dragging her. The more she resisted, the more the thing in her mouth dug in. She was pulled out of the water, until she was hanging over the beast. She writhed in terror, but it was no good, she couldn't escape. The unfamiliar heat of the sun burnt her big dorsal fin as she dangled, helpless. She felt the slimy touch of the parasites grabbing her body with their tentacles. Water cascaded off her glistening body as she was lifted higher. Her gills convulsed as she struggled to breath in the thick hot air.

She thrashed about with all the energy she had left, though her gills were burning. More tentacles grabbed at her, making her nauseous. She had to save her babies. So in one final convulsion, she used all her muscles, and parasites' soft flesh let go. Then something hard and rough collapsed and she thrashed against the beast's body. Then she was flying, landing with a splash in the water. The pressure in her mouth was gone. She was free.

She swam quickly away, although her panic disorientated her. Days passed as she refocussed on getting to the nursery. She tried to forget about the beast with its grasping claws and the parasites with their sticky tentacles. But she was also ravenous with hunger, and the mighty beasts always hunted the largest fish shoals.

Up ahead, in the distance, a dull throb again vibrated, along with the sounds of thousands of fish in distress. She tasted blood and fear and death. She swam closer, hungry. This could be the big meal she needed. But the signals were confusing. If the throbbing came from a beast, it sounded bigger than anything she'd heard before. At the same time, it was gliding around a huge shoal. She hesitated, unsure what to do, until hunger and the flipping and twirling of her babies inside her drove her forward. Their lives depended on her.

The beast was indeed the biggest yet. Fish thrashed atop its belly. But her senses buzzed with something else too. Ghostly shapes sunk slowly in front of her. An electric current radiated through the water, so full of pain and terror that it hurt her sensors. The shapes were bodies – of her own kind. Alive but motionless. She couldn't understand why they were sinking helplessly to the bottom. Why weren't they swimming?

But then she tasted their blood too. It poured out of gashes in their sides. They had no fins with which to swim. Soon the sandy floor was littered with their prone bodies, their gills pumping as they tried to suck in oxygen. They couldn't breathe if they couldn't swim. The parasites on this giant beast had eaten their fins, then dropped them back in the ocean to drown. Sickened by this madness, she began to swim away. She had to reach her nursery.

But another of the great billowing beasts was coming towards her, and she felt an unmistakeable pressure, as if she would be drawn to its mouth, where its teeth would slash off her fins, leaving her a helpless torso on the seabed. Though tired and hungry, she gathered all her strength and fought off the beast's pull, resisting its suction bit by bit, swimming as hard as she could, until the pressure relented.

She swam away then in a panic, until she could no longer hear the beast's basal throbbing, or sense the death throes of her fellows. Where was she now? She was back where she had bitten that disgusting parasite. She was going in circles, getting no closer to the nursery, or to a meal. The world that she used to dominate had turned upside down, frustrating her every move. She would never give up of course, the draw of the nursery was built into her brain, an instinct that she could not ignore. She just had to settle her senses.

The twisting inside her belly gave her no respite. It was hard to think straight, yet she had to make progress. It was her duty as a mother. She could hardly believe it when she detected that noise again, the low throb of a beast, and the overwhelming smell of blood. This time she sensed large chunks of fish flesh floating on the surface, just next to the beast. These beasts were so dangerous, yet she was also starving, her strength almost gone.

A frenzy for food overtook her. She approached the thing from behind, careful to avoid its cruel cutting tail. She couldn't see its mouth busy in the water. She also found fish flesh floating around its sides. Fresh. Sumptuous. She opened her mouth and took a bite, slowly. There was no pain, no pulling. She took another bite. She gorged on the blood and fish until her stomach stopped gnawing.

She sensed him before she saw him. A large male swooped towards her. She darted away, his jaws just missing her body. She didn't care, her stomach was full at last. And she knew now – she was nearly at the nursery. This time nothing would get in her way. She left him with the fish flesh, and swam away.

An explosion, followed by a pulse of sound and water, suddenly propelled her forward. Lumps of flesh rained down around her. She grabbed a piece and swallowed it, then almost coughed it back up. It was the male that had just swooped her. Somehow, he had been instantly carved into small pieces.

She had no time to think how. Guided by the earth's magnetism, she was finally at the nursery. She glided through the soft leaves of seaweed, hidden from view, and felt tension leaving her body. Nothing could see her here. This was a place for females, undiscovered by the beasts. As her body relaxed, so did her babies. They wriggled through her cloaca and, for a few seconds, explored their new watery world; then they disappeared into the soft caress of seaweed. Her duty was done. She would never see them again, never know if they lived or died.

But their absence did have one advantage – her focus need not be on the nursey anymore. It was time for her to return to the hunt.

ABOUT 'THE GREAT FISH'

My story 'The Great Fish' challenges the tired old trope of the shark as malevolent monster, driven by nothing more than a desire for human blood. There are countless examples in popular culture, among the most well-know is the novel *Jaws* by Peter Benchley, later turned into a famous movie by Steven Spielberg.

But there are plenty of other examples on film: *Deep Blue Sea, The Meg, The Shallows, The Reef, Open Water, In the Deep* and others.

Seventy-five per cent of ocean shark species are now facing extinction. The reality is that the shark is the victim, not the villain. My story attempts to redress the balance, showing sharks as creatures simply going about their business in an ocean invaded by humans. The shark encounters man-made barriers on her journey, including a giant factory ship killing hundreds of sharks just for their fins, highlighting the inequity of revenge hunts for sharks when one human is killed.

ABOUT SUE OSBORNE

Sue Osborne lives in north-west Sydney with her husband and two grown-up daughters. She works in communication and journalism. In 2020, she completed a Masters of Creative Writing at Macquarie University, and has now been writing short stories for several years. She has been shortlisted for the national Furphy Literary Awards three times, with a story published in their anthology in 2020, 2021 and 2022. She was also shortlisted for the Northern Beaches Writers Competition in 2023.

MYTH OR REAL

———cvɔ———

HOWARD REID

Ten Questions to Find Out: Terrorist or Freedom Fighter?

INTRODUCTION

The floor manager counted down, "Five, four, three…" then held up silent fingers to gesture 'two' and 'one', before swishing his index finger to indicate that they were now on air.

"Welcome!" Morty beamed with a smile, turning from a side camera towards the main camera in the studio's centre. "I'm your host Morty Jansen, and tonight I'm joined by a man determined to set the record straight. What he perceives to be a documentary, we have long believed to be a famous action movie. But he was the getaway driver the night of the robbery in question, and he insists that his friend never fell to his death from the thirtieth floor of the that Plaza building in Los Angeles on Christmas Eve 1988! He insists that his friend is still alive, and is in fact quite upset with his ongoing portrayal as a terrorist. This common portrayal of action movie villains is so rife, he says, it has affected his own biographical depiction in what we will now call The Film.

"So, myth, legend or the story of a flesh-and-blood man? Tonight we ask the hard-hitting questions to find out."

QUESTION 1

Morty turned to his guest, not without his fair share of nerves. "Welcome, Herr Gunter. I thought your 'friend' was dead?"

Herr Gunter shifted in his seat and attempted a smile. "Thank you, Morty, and greetings to you and your audience. Let me start by assuring you that news of my friend's death has been greatly exaggerated. The robbery at the Plaza certainly took place, but he did not fall from the thirtieth floor. No one could survive such a fall, how ridiculous. No, he *escaped* the building with a good number of bearer bonds. How much the bonds were worth, and where we hid them while making our escape, is not something I will be talking about, so please refrain from asking. Compared to what we missed out on, it was a pitiful amount. As for the scene with my dear friend Herr–"

"Remember, no real names!" Morty quickly interrupted.

"Fine. As for the scene with my dear friend 'Han' falling to his death, it was pure Hollywood invention. Smoke and mirrors. Better everyone believed he was dead than worry the community. Did anyone actually see him hit the ground? Something fell from the tower, yes. There was the sound of a thud on the movie, but no visual. Was there a body to be seen? Any close-ups?

"A better story for the police was that he was dead, that we all were. The community could now exhale their deep breaths. But we are very much alive." The way he said 'alive' sounded like a threat.

Morty glanced around the studio. The audience was silent. The crew were silent. Gunter's serious demeanour was clearly both alarming and fascinating everyone.

QUESTION 2

He glanced at his research sheet. "So, Herr Gunter, are you…" How could he phrase this so as not to offend the man? "From what my team tells me, you'd like us to understand that The Film was a biography of sorts, of key events in your friend's life. And one of the reasons you're here today is to clarify some… errors?"

"That is correct."

"Thank you, um," Morty stumbled, "Herr Gunter. Please go on."

"Yes, well, The Film is close to reality on many levels. We planned and executed a high-class robbery. The rest of our team was mercilessly killed. The building was unfortunately blown up. Something fell or was pushed out of a window in the tower, though it was not Han. I also survived. Neither of us are 'movie characters' – as you can clearly see, I am sitting here with you, so I am very much alive, and living a comparatively quiet life. So much of The Film is indubitably true, but some is not. And of course the tone is off."

Morty's earpiece buzzed.

"Go hard early," the floor manager said in a whisper.

Morty glanced at her warily. It was alright for her, clutching a clipboard, hiding behind the cameras. He was right there. Still, this was his job. He cleared his throat and pretended to read from his research sheet. "On that note, Herr Gunter, while losing your team must have been very hard… with all due respect, viewers might find it hard to sympathise after the callous nature with which your friend disposed of the plaza's chief executive. Some might even argue that The Film's tone, portraying you and your friends as villains, was deserved. What would you say to such a viewer? Is this how you and Han have always lived, with such apparent indifference between life and death, removing any person in your path? What of your childhoods? Was this desire to eliminate any human obstruction, someone blocking your path, a part of your life growing up?"

Gunter leant back in his chair and steepled his fingertips, seeming to ponder the question, or which violent act he would inflict on Morty for asking it. "Our childhoods were fine," he said eventually. "Han and I lived in Rüdesheim on the Rhine River. It is very scenic. The river is used for touring riverboats, transporting goods up and down the waterway. The town is surrounded by vineyards, it's very pretty. Siegfried's Mechanical Music Museum is a prime tourist attraction, with an extensive collection of automated musical instruments in Germany. I believe it was the first museum of its type in Germany.

"Han's family was particularly musical, none of which is portrayed in The Film. He learnt various string instruments in his youth. He also liked completing various types of puzzles – all types of jigsaws, scientific experiments, and mathematical puzzles. We used to enjoy reading mystery books, gathering clues and seeing if we could guess the outcome." He smirked and gazed into the distance, like he was remembering something specific.

He didn't care to share the memory. "We also liked making models that related to our favourite mysteries – planes, cities, trains. We enjoyed trips to cities to find new puzzles. We'd scour all the second-hand puzzle shops, book and model shops we could find. People in Rüdesheim, which is more of a village than a town I suppose, were particularly kind in lending us model kits, puzzle books and jigsaws."

Morty nodded, intent on appearing interested.

"So you can see," Gunter said slowly, making eye contact with Morty, "the story of Han's childhood presented in The Film was entirely concocted, and planted in our personal files – held by the then West German government – to distance us from a watershed moment in our own lives.

"Han's early life, as portrayed in The Film," he sneered, then looked directly into the camera, "is an official creation to mask the real nature of our youth. The so-called capture of his father – who was supposedly given the profession of a publisher conscript in the Wehrmacht, then captured during the war's last exchanges and sent to a Russian prison camp – is entirely untrue. He was 'conscripted' to a so-called 'volunteer' group in Rüdesheim. How you can be a 'conscripted volunteer' is beyond me. He also did not travel with his mother Elsa and brother Simon to East Berlin.

"Rather he lived with his older brother Simon, you will have heard of him, enjoying a simple life with his parents, who were both musicians. *Competent* musicians in fact. His mother played piano and sung, while his father played violin and other stringed instruments. My parents owned the hall where they often performed. They were not of a level strong enough to join a major orchestra, but they had a solid following through the festivals they played, and small shows for visiting groups of tourists. They were prominent players in local regional orchestras. Money was tight but he had a happy and creative childhood. Then…" Gunter paused.

"And then?" Morty asked.

"Then one day," Gunter leant forward in his seat, "Han's mother was attacked while walking home from a concert that Han's parents had given in the village. Han, his brother and I were helping our fathers pack up so they could speak with audience members, while our mothers started to walk home. It was a robbery that did not go to plan. Han and I rushed to their aid as soon as we heard their screams, and were able to fight off the attackers, who fled. The cowards. All but one. We tackled him to the ground, and he would have lived if not for the stone. It sliced his head open, shaped as it was like the edge of a knife.

"He died within minutes. Han was arrested for it of course, being the person who drove his head into the rock." Another sneer. He moved his hands to grip his armrests. "The other thieves were arrested and convicted. But *Han* was charged with using undue force. Served six months in a juvenile detention facility! Then, after Han was released, it was under a good behaviour bond for three years, or he would have to return to prison for a further term. Once the three-year period was up, the offence was removed from his legal records. Many people spoke up for Han – given he himself was a musician of promise, a diligent student – but none of that helped his mother of course.

"She had never hurt anyone. She didn't deserve to die.

"And she wasn't the only one. While he was locked up, Han read a lot and found others like us – innocent people just minding their own business, then persecuted by government nonsense. And yes, Han found groups of individuals fighting for freedom. In The Film, his supposed 'character' mentions groups such as the Volksfrei Movement and Asian Dawn – these are the type of groups we had great sympathy for, but never did they indoctrinate or brainwash us. We found our way to them. Where we could, we helped them move towards their goals, whatever they considered to be their 'Holy Grail', because whether they were right or wrong they were fighting for their definition of freedom."

Gunter stared into the camera a moment, then leaned back in his seat again, and glanced at Morty to indicate he had finished speaking.

"Okay." Morty gave him a nod, unsure what he intended that to mean. "But why turn your mind and actions to supporting rebels who, some would say, included people no better than merciless killers looking for wealth and power? Could you not see past the horrifying experience you suffered in your youth? You are both clearly highly intelligent and cultured men, minds with the propensity to try out new things, of working out solutions to problems, which could have given you a bright and possibly well-paid future. As educated men, you could have advanced a post-war Germany."

Gunter pursed his lips, thinking.

Morty waited.

Gunter seemed to draw out the moment, as if slowly loading a gun with bullets. One after the other, after the other. "I suppose," he said eventually, "we could have put the incident with our mothers, and the man Han killed, behind us. However, for the short time we spent in detention, it allowed us to read about so many people subjected to tyranny. Corrupt governments stealing from their people, deciding to arbitrarily wipe out ethnicities to 'purify' their country, pressuring businesses to force workers into long hours and drive down wages. They prey on the poor and middle class – who else is going to stop them? We left detention believing we *had* to fight for oppressed people. It was our destiny.

"In your country, Australia, you have an iconic bushranger, Ned Kelly, often celebrated for doing the same. *He* was a lawbreaker and a killer. He started a life of crime by opposing police when *his* mother was falsely accused of stealing a horse. The dice was thrown for Kelly, as it was for both of us, and the numbers that came up set us on our path. We had no choice in it."

QUESTION 5

Morty took a deep breath. What Gunter was saying, it sounded… reasonable. Yet he had to remember who this man was, what he had done. "This all sounds very understandable, Herr Gunter, but people know you for your disruption of life and several murders, including assassinations of high-level government figures. As your life progressed, were you really still trying to help the 'oppressed'?" His hand signalled inverted commas to give emphasis to his point.

Gunter took another excruciating pause. "The thing is, Morty, Han and I found so many groups willing to pay for our services, that we found we could make a decent living, and send money home to our families. I think that, like many people who start off as purists trying to assist the downtrodden, whoever they may be, and where ever they may be, we simply became… misdirected. Some of the regional or national groups we tried to help, were not actually representing the interests of the movement they claimed to represent. They were seeking personal gain or power, not the espoused goals of a righteous movement. But by then it was too late. Our convictions did begin wavering, and that's when Han and I found a new motivation to theirs: money. Everybody needs money."

"Alright." Morty straightened his back. Now they were getting somewhere. "So let's return then to your families, specifically to Han's brother Simon, who we meet in a sequel to The Film. You said that Han and Simon got on well as children. After their mother died, did their relationship change? Simon claims that his robbery was in part to avenge *your* failure."

Gunter narrowed his eyes at Morty. "Must I repeat myself? I've already said that Han and I both enjoyed our childhoods. The incident with our mothers affected us both, of course it did – how much, I don't know, especially for Han and Simon. Simon was never committed to reform like Han and I, not as interested in supporting the oppressed. After his mother passed, he did once tell me that if he wanted something he would take it, if he could not get whatever he wanted by legal means.

"Stupid as the robbers were that day, he told me he saw in their eyes the same need, the wanting to acquire something they did not have." Gunter shook his head in disapproval and looked down at his lap. A touch of melancholy spread across his hardened face. "I did not see it but he did. Perhaps it was osmosis, Simon developing some affinity with the thieves. He took offence more easily after that, at any slight against him or the family. He had never excelled at school and, though interested in music, did not play well. But as childhood friends, we always had time for each other, and he loved his brother."

Morty exchanged looks with the floor manager. Were they finally getting to see a softer side to these criminals?

Gunter went on. "Did you know there's an alternative ending to that sequel?" He raised his eyebrows at Morty. "Where Han's brother and that pesky American cop," he rolls his lips in disgust, "face off in an apparent version of a game, a sort of Russian roulette. Pure Hollywood fantasy of course. The ending as released is accurate. I don't know whether avenging our failure was part of Simon's motivation, but I know Han misses him today and every day."

QUESTION 7

"What of the rest of your gang?" Morty asked quickly, hoping to snare Gunter in a vulnerable moment. "Where did you meet them? Did any of them carry the same conviction as you and Han, about liberating the downtrodden?"

Gunter smiled, his eyes glinting as if seeing straight through Morty. "Some of our group had the same ideas. Others were poor criminals with no interest in anything other than being rich. I met almost all of them through engagements, generally in the Middle East, while a few I met during European operations. This included my number two, a very reliable man. My programmer was a local hacker, known to the FBI. Our concierge was a disenchanted ex-marine.

"Some of our group were in opposition to our ideals when we met, but they soon listened to how we could make money together. There's nothing like telling someone who could shoot you at any moment that you know how they could get rich.

"You know, when The Film was released in Germany they changed all the gang's names to English names and made us Irish terrorists."

QUESTION 8

"Fascinating!" Morty grinned. "And what about now? What of Han's place in today's culture? He has been rated – on a variety of websites – as one of the greatest villains of all time. There are websites selling memorabilia of him, lamps and furniture modelled on the Plaza and his 'fall'." He hand-signalled inverted commas again to prevent offence. "There is even debate as to whether The Film is an appropriate Christmas movie. Does Han see himself as a cultural icon?"

Gunter tilted his head, staring at Morty. "I have seen the different sites you mention. These so-called rating sites use highly subjective criteria, seemingly the basis of American humour. Memorabilia, toys – all a waste of time. This is not culture. It is rubbish produced by vultures. I've seen the slogans too. The Film was never about Christmas. There was a party, the chief executive was there, I and the rest of our group thought there was a chance he would help Han open the safe to save his people; but we were also prepared if he didn't, as was the case.

Nothing festive about it. You want culture? Listen to Beethoven, Schumann or Brahms. Listen to Dietrich Fischer-Dieskau and Sandra sing classical and contemporary. Read Bertolt Brecht, Jenny Erpenbeck, or her grandmother Hedda Zinner. They and others are a part of German culture."

QUESTION 9

Morty gave Gunter a 'fair enough' look, then saw the floor manager giving him a 'wrap it up' signal. "Herr Gunter, we're coming to the end of our time together now, and I'd like to ask about your and Han's lives now. I estimate your age to be late seventies. How do you both fill your time? What do notorious villains, robbers, killers do in the final stages of their life?"

"Final stages?" Gunter scoffed. "You seem about the same age as me – are you in the final stages of your life?"

Morty shifted in his seat. They had shared such personal moments and yet... Was that a threat?

Gunter shrugged. "Han and I live simply. We have enough money. We don't travel much. Han spends most of his time in the forest, hunting game. Sometimes we frequent the seaside. If I appear older than I am, that's because I don't want to draw attention to myself. Maybe I use a walker, but maybe I don't need to. I keep my hat pulled down." Gunter laughed at what he thought was a good joke.

No one else laughed.

Morty chuckled for the sake of politeness. "Well, thank you so much Herr Gunter for your time. Enjoy your seaside and hunting. And, just in case we have viewers who'd rather not bump into you or Han in the forest, where exactly do you live now?"

"Well, I'm pleased to hear you believe Han and I are alive, Morty, not just movie characters after all. As to where we live, if indeed there is a 'we' and I am not simply 'me'." Gunter straightened his body and motioned for a camera operator to approach him with their camera. Once the operator came close enough that Gunter's face filled the lens and the screens of monitors all around the studio, Gunter glared then whispered with the intimacy of a murderer. "In the time it's taken for me to give this interview, in the time it's taken for viewers to watch it or read its transcript, I will certainly be living exactly and precisely where I've always wanted to live – within your mind. Yippee ki yay, m–"

"Go to black!" called the floor manager.

But already the studio was filling with Gunter's manic and incandescent laughter. It reminded Morty of how Han himself had laughed in The Film. Perhaps the two men had spent a little too much time together. Or perhaps no time at all.

ABOUT 'MYTH OR REAL'

The 'criminal mastermind' archetype usually involves a seemingly invincible villain with an impenetrable plan. It's commonly used in action stories to justify the development of the lead protagonist. Such villains can, however, garner hero status from their followers, as well as from readers, through their charismatic personas and ingenious actions. My story attempts to reference these impressive villains, such as Hans Grubber from *Die Hard* and the Joker from the *Batman* saga.

ABOUT HOWARD REID

Howard Reid has authored/co-authored twelve previous books. In addition, he has been involved in authoring television scripts, research reports and a wide variety of educational publications for both government and the private sector over a period of more than forty years. His first novel *Street Cleaner* was released in April 2023. This is his second story published in an anthology by NBWG.

CIRCE

⌁

ELISE ROBERTSON

"Don't eat the food!" Odysseus warned. "It has been prepared by Circe, the great sorceress of Aenea!"

One of the men spat out a mouthful, flinging away the bread from which he had just taken a ragged bite.

"Really, Odysseus?" I snapped. "My reputation has always been bleak. But that is a bit dark, even for me."

The men surveyed the feast spread out upon the table with wide hungry eyes. Fresh juicy grapes. Meltingly soft cheese. A massive haunch of lamb, dripping with fat. It would be a blessed change from the meagre, monotonous ship's fare of hard cheese and salted pork.

"I cannot extend my hospitality, my protection to you, if you do not eat."

Odysseus toyed with a fork, his expression as dark as his curly hair and the beard shadowing his firm jaw.

"Or drink," I added sharply.

Odysseus's shrewd brown eyes narrowed at me, then

scrutinised his crew. Their beards damp, their cups drained to the dregs. "I warned all of you. This is Circe!" Odysseus growled.

I withdrew a slender magical rod of stone-pine from the folds of my silver silk gown and aimed it at the closest man. At once, the man corrupted into a wolf – his broad-chested body shrinking, collapsing onto all fours, sprouting sleek grey fur, his ears flattening back as his mouth elongated into a powerful snout. I jabbed my wand at the next man, who morphed into a white-haired goat – stooped body shrinking rapidly, his brown eyes darting about warily. I struck my wand at the third man whose tall, thin body exploded sideways into the form of a corpulent pig – greedy belly almost dragging on the ground.

One by one, each member of Odysseus's crew shifted into animal form. Soon we were surrounded by a small menagerie of strange animals – barking, braying, snapping, and grunting in distress.

"I see little difference." I drank my wine, savouring each delicious mouthful. "Do you not want my hospitality, Odysseus?"

Odysseus glared at me, then sipped his wine. His body rippled slightly but refused to reveal his true animal form. Too late I noticed the sprig of moly folded into the drape of Odysseus's cotton tunic. Of course!

Odysseus met my eyes with an intense stare and his soft mouth relaxed into a wide mischievous smile.

My forehead pinched with irritation. Only a god would know of moly. Who would have the nerve to send him thus armed to my hidden island in the Mediterranean? The gold lyre brooch winked up at me from Odysseus's tunic. It had to be Hermes! The god of trade, travellers, and thieves.

I leaned over the table, refilling Odysseus's goblet from a silver pitcher, aware that my gown pressed tightly against my skin. I gazed down at Odysseus's thin tunic sculpted enticingly to his muscled arms. "To your health," I announced, raising my goblet.

Odysseus's eyes flicked toward my chest, then swiftly looked away. I sat up straighter, a smile on my lips.

"To your hospitality," he agreed. His warm eyes then gazed intensely into my face. Smiling, Odysseus tipped back his cup and drained every last drop.

"Do you think your wife has taken a lover while you're gone?" I asked.

For the past year, questions such as these had hung between us like a knife waiting to fall.

"No, Circe, I do not. Nor do I care to think on it – the idea is ridiculous."

I held my breath, allowing a sudden flash of anger to register on my usually mask-like face. Odysseus's unquestioning faith in his wife angered and disturbed me. Strangely, I also felt a pang of sadness for her – the certainty with which Odysseus regarded her propriety.

I snorted. "Only a man would think something so natural ridiculous!"

Odysseus looked away.

Silence again; long and uncomfortable.

Men were so blind to their treatment of women and Odysseus was no different. My lip curled in distaste. "What was that pathetic fight you said Menelaus and Achilles had over a woman? About who had a greater claim to her?"

Odysseus ignored me, shrugging off his tunic, tempting me with his lithe tanned body.

I bit the inside of my mouth, stifling a scream of frustration. At Odysseus. At the world. These pious dutiful women were revered and rewarded by the gods and society. Silent, blindly obedient, and uncomplaining; without desires or fears of their own. Even Hera, wife of the great Zeus, was expected to turn a blind eye as he scattered his seed to the wind. Dutiful Hera was expected to keep her legs crossed. How could women bear it?

"You should return home, Odysseus." I should have said so well before now. I turned away from him, a dozen emotions flickering through my mind. Jealousy and pity towards his wife Penelope. Anger at Odysseus's fickleness and power over me. Acute sadness and resentment about possibly letting him go. But the fact remained that his wife and son would always be there, between us.

Odysseus shook his head, squeezing my hand with reassurance. "My father, Laertes, and my son Telemachus will be more than capable of ruling in my stead."

I pulled my hand away. "An old man and a boy?"

"It has been twelve years today since I left. Soon Telemachus will be a grown man of his own," he affirmed with a smile.

"Twelve years is a long time, Odysseus. They will think you killed in the war."

Odysseus shook his head, determined on unlacing my bodice.

"The longer you are gone, the more difficult it will be to deny what's happened between us," I warned.

Odysseus ignored my words and focused instead on kissing my neck.

I released a sigh of desire and frustration. "Your wife may have even started to believe it herself."

Odysseus raised his head from my neck and frowned, his dark eyes deep in thought. In the year he'd been here with me, this was the first time he seemed unsure of himself.

"What if some advisors poison Telemachus against his mother, try to win him to their side? Perhaps even gain his favour with gifts." I knew in my heart all these things were likely. It made me press on and say what Odysseus needed to hear. For his own sake. "Or they might kill him, if he becomes too powerful."

"None of that will happen," Odysseus growled, his fist clenching the bedsheets as though strangling unseen enemies.

"These same men might court your wife," I continued, trailing my fingers down Odysseus's firm chest. "She will resist, at first. But for how long?"

Odysseus scowled.

"None such men will suffer a woman to rule for long," I

said, lips tight. My eyes burned with tears, as I pushed away memories of days lounging with Odysseus by the fire, discussing philosophy and the strengths and weakness of the Greek city-states, and other such topics usually reserved for conversation between men. We'd snuggled close to one another. Odysseus never once talked over me or patronised me with a pitying smile, but had listened to me. Really listened, as though what I had to say was precious to him.

"Circe–"

"Go home, Odysseus," I sighed, slipping out of our warm bed. "Before it's too late for you. For your family."

⌇

The wind wailed as I stood on the cliff, overlooking the churning sea, watching as Odysseus and his men, no longer in animal form, sailed away. I inhaled deeply, taking in Odysseus's musky scent lingering on my clothing from our last embrace, mixed with the chilled, salty air.

Another massive wave pounded against the rocky cliff below me and I rubbed the lapis lazuli amulet hanging from my neck and recited a quick prayer.

"O Athena! Goddess of Strategy. Hear my plight. Lend me your Owl-like hearing and sight."

I poured a libation of wine upon the altar in front of me. The wine sizzled then sank into the soapstone, staining it a delicious red. Anxious minutes past as I waited, then a thrill of joy shivered

134

down my back as, looking out at the sea, I could now see the men bustling about the deck of the ship with acute clarity.

"Com-pany!" Odysseus ordered, his familiar husky voice ringing with authority. "Row... Row... Row... Row."

Odysseus sat at the stern, keeping time for the men; the steady slap of leather against the drum an eerie and unflinching heartbeat urging the crew on.

I swallowed a sob. Although being alone was usually a welcome prospect to me, losing Odysseus felt like losing a part of myself.

Suddenly, a massive shadow loomed over the ship, blocking its path. Scylla's lips sneered back from each of her six reptilian heads, each mouth crowded with rows of needle-sharp teeth, guarded with four dagger-like fangs. Her six heads extended on long, scaly necks from a wide body armoured with scales. Encircling her waist were four Mastiff dog-heads, growling and snapping.

I shuddered. I had warned Odysseus that facing Scylla would be the most prudent choice of the two monsters inhabiting the waters near my shores; but on seeing her sharp fangs and near impenetrable scales, I began to reconsider.

"Men!" Odysseus yelled. "Arm yourselves!"

Those men closest to Scylla fell over each other in their haste to get away. The rest of the crew either continued rowing or notched an arrow to their drawn bows with no fear of death on their faces.

Scylla's first head lunged faster than a whip at one of the

soldiers, her fangs ripping into the man's neck. The man lurched backward, tumbling over the side with a heavy splash into the heaving waves.

My stomach clenched, every vein in my body alert with fear.

"Fire at will!" Odysseus shouted. The other men took up the cry and directed their arrows towards the first head.

Within seconds, dozens of arrows bristled from Scylla's scaled neck, ribbons of blood trickling down. Scylla's first head still struck out at the men, though not nearly as lightning-fast as before, almost clumsily, allowing the soldiers to easily evade her snapping jaws.

Several sailors climbed the rigging; a knife or axe handle braced in their mouth.

Scylla's second head tossed a man yelling in terror into the air and slammed him face-first onto the deck with a hard thump.

Odysseus wove between fighting soldiers and barrels of salted fish, his lithe body always moving. To pause or slow would mean certain death.

Spears broke against Scylla's jewel-hard scales. Scylla struck back, three of her heads darting towards a knot of soldiers. The soldiers flung up their shields, her vicious jaws puncturing the bronze sheeting with hail-sized dents.

I bit back a shout, and dug my nails into my thigh.

"She wants me. I'll tackle her heads. Aim for her neck and belly!" Odysseus commanded, hurling a spear straight at Scylla's closest neck.

With another scream, Scylla's wounded head shot out at

Odysseus. I flinched, my hand covering my mouth. Odysseus dodged it, rolling swiftly out of reach. Scylla struck again, this time with her second head, slamming into Odysseus's shoulder, her knife-sharp fangs tearing into his shield-arm.

Fear gripped my heart and squeezed. Odysseus clutched his ruined arm – a significant amount of flesh had been ripped away.

"No!" I cried fiercely.

The wind snatched my outburst, the echo stretching eerily across the expanse of the strait.

Suddenly, Scylla twisted around, and her twelve brilliant eyes locked on mine. "Witch!" the monster snarled.

I froze.

When I looked again, I could see a woman with shiny golden hair spilling to her trim waist – a young woman I'd trapped in a monstrous form, many years ago. The image distorted. Only her multitude of eyes remained the same; a beautiful sea-glass green. What in Hades had I done?

Her eyes burned with unvented rage. My breath faltered.

"Scylla!" I pleaded. "Spare him and I promise…" What did I think I was going to say? That it was a terrible mistake and I'd change her back?

But I had meant it back then. Oh, I had meant it. And there was no changing that now.

"Why should I trust you, witch?" Scylla asked. "You took everything from me!" Her voice from the six mouths rose to a piercing pitch, making my head pound. "Your very touch is poison!"

Guilt squirmed in my stomach and bile welled in my tight throat. I shuddered as I remembered the way Scylla had screamed as my potion seared her flawless, pale skin, when she'd bathed in the usually crystal-clear stream I'd made seethe an unnatural emerald-green. Her dazzling smile, her generous breasts and hips that were so irresistible to Glaucus. Glaucus, a weak-willed man turned immortal sea-god, who I'd wanted as my lover. Who took one startled look at Scylla's drastically altered appearance and fled into the sea.

Had I made the same terrible mistake with Odysseus? I glanced back at him. My vision blurred with tears.

No. It was not the same at all. Odysseus was going home to his wife and children. Odysseus was never meant for me.

Scylla's lantern-like eyes took in Odysseus, bent in bloodied agony, then quickly glanced back to my pained face.

"Ha!" Her voice was harsh as a dog's bark. "True love. How *fragile*."

My insight into human nature was my gift and my curse. Misery *needs* company. I knew in that moment, Scylla would not cease until she had killed Odysseus before my eyes. It was like looking in a mirror. Monsters aren't born; they are created. Brutalized and abandoned by those around them until only ugliness remains. Bitter, suspicious, every action of others considered a threat.

Odysseus tried to pick up his shield but dropped it immediately with a cry. All six of Scylla's heads smiled coldly. It was clear Odysseus no longer had the strength to defend himself.

"Eurylochus! Acacius! Kyros! To me!" Odysseus shouted urgently.

My heart leaped seeing his courage and bravery.

A square-faced, stocky man and two identical gracefully lean men raced towards Odysseus. The twins faced outward, on either side from Odysseus, their swords raised. As one of Scylla's heads reared forward again, Acacius and Eurylochus threw a fishing net over it. As Scylla's second and third head and neck entwined, twisting and thrashing in the net, Odysseus hacked at the second neck with his sharp sword. He winced and swore as he struck again and again. On the seventh blow, the severed head fell to the deck, where it continued to twitch and writhe like a freshly caught fish.

I clasped my hands with a breath of hope – Scylla had only four of her six heads remaining.

With a gnashing cry, Scylla's teeth sliced through the net, her third head exploding forward at Odysseus. Odysseus staggered backward, avoiding Scylla's strike, catching the mast for support as he collapsed to his knees. Scylla slithered forward until she was a few inches from Odysseus's prone body, grinning in triumph.

"I'm going to enjoy eating you Odyss-sseus..." Scylla crowed. "Alive!"

"Odysseus!" I screamed.

Scylla lunged for the kill and Odysseus plunged his blade into Scylla's mid-section, right up to the hilt. Scylla's four remaining heads screamed at the sword quivering in her stomach.

Odysseus smiled triumphantly, then wrenched the sword out

of Scylla's body. Scylla gave a shrill cry, the mastiff dogs sprouting from her waist howled in despair – the wound was a fatal one.

While my face blazed with anger, a small smile tugged at my dry mouth. Of course! When Odysseus got backed into a corner, he always used his wits to escape his opponent. The mad farmer ploughing with salt. The wooden Trojan horse whose belly was filled with warriors. Polyphemus the Cyclops, blinded and outwitted by 'Nobody'. I was at once impressed at Odysseus's cleverness and furious at myself for not seeing through his daring rouse.

Odysseus held his sword out in front of him, tensing for the next attack. Sweat poured down his forehead. His olive skin had turned pale. His tunic was stained crimson from the gaping wound in his left arm, and his breeches too, from the deep wound in his thigh.

"Curse you, Odysseus!" Scylla spat, her lips twisting with disgust. "Curse you, Circe! How terribly alike you are! Unfeeling. Treacherous." Suddenly, her flat green eyes gleamed with savage joy. "I will leave you at the mercy of my sisss-ter," Scylla hissed. "What goes around, comes around, and around, and around."

Scylla's spiteful laughter rang in my ears as she sank into the seething red sea and my newly won hope plunged into terror.

Odysseus limped back to his place at the stern. "Comp-any! Row!" he roared.

The men rushed to their benches as the sea churned. The ship began to pitch, rolling, rising, and plunging like a frightened horse. Rough waves spilled over the sides, swamping the men. A massive vortex had opened up like a sinkhole. Deep in the centre was an enormous mouth like a sea urchin, sucking in the sea. The gurgling sluice of draining water sounded like a cavernous growl.

My stomach swooped. It was Charybdis, the terrible sea snake. Scylla could be deadly, but no hero had ever escaped Charybdis's clutches.

I clasped my hands to my beating heart as Odysseus's ship was caught in Charybdis's pull, whirling faster and faster, spiraling towards the mouth of the funnel. Planks of wood, wreckage from lost ships, splintered into the ship's hull with brutal force, making the ship shudder. The faster the ship spun, the more difficult it became for the crew to weave around the debris. As the ship teetered dangerously, I swore, hoping the ship wouldn't capsize.

The men rowed desperately. They didn't have the strength to claw their way out of the monster's grip. Not alone. Not without my help.

I stood and concentrated on slowing my breathing, feeling my bare feet connect with the earth; imagining my legs were roots, strong and deep. I ignored the agitated shouts of the soldiers and moans of the dying.

I tapped my wand onto the altar before me, and a plump sheep with trailing white wool materialised, its live body curled obediently across the stone. It was the most precious of my flock.

"O Athena! Goddess of wise counsel, and champion of Greek soldiers. Hear my prayer. Send aid to free them from Charybdis thrall."

Another flick of my wand and bright emerald-green flames burst forth, consuming the sheep on the altar. The sheep shimmered strangely; diaphanous, like smoke. Slowly, the animal dissolved until it was no more.

As the minutes past, I envisioned Odysseus's ship dashed to pieces in the whirlpool and being swiftly devoured by Charybdis's cruel maw. Then my hair floated upward with a nebulous shimmer and billowed backwards, carried on a strong chilled wind, sweeping away the ashes of the spell.

Athena had accepted my offering!

I looked to the sea. The ship banked hard, scaling the sheer cliff of water, the sail buoyed by the fresh wind, then the ship burst out the other side of the vortex. The crew's backs were hunched and their shoulders strained as they rowed to safety, the beat of their oars never failing despite the exhaustion on their faces.

At last, having put a significant distance between the ship and the monsters, the crew erupted into jubilant hoarse cheers. Odysseus limped past the men, slapping his fellow warriors heartily on the back as he returned to the stern. Sitting down once more, he glanced towards my cliffs, looked back at me with a cheeky grin and winked.

Tears of relief coursed down my cheeks as I fell exhausted to my knees and clasped my chest, muttering. "I am strong enough to take this. I am strong. I am enough." Words I needed to remind myself, for I was not only the powerful Circe, but a woman too.

I fumbled in the pouch circling my waist and sprinkled a

handful of monkshood petals and crushed black tourmaline onto the altar.

"O Hecate! Mother of mine, Goddess of sorcery, and watcher of crossroads. Take the wounds of Odysseus. Let his pain be my pain."

I doubled over with sudden dizziness and pain. My trembling hand came away from the bloodied mangled stump of my left arm.

For once I had done the right thing, so why did I feel as though the air had been stamped from my lungs? Why had emptiness and despair crushed my heart?

"Fool!" I muttered and stared at the ship disappearing over the horizon. "He isn't meant for you. They are never meant for you."

ABOUT 'CIRCE'

My story 'Circe' is a retelling of the epic myth *The Odyssey* by Homer, retold from the point-of-view of the villainous enchantress Circe. Circe represents the villain archetype of the bully, an antagonist who frightens and harasses the hero emotionally and sometimes physically. Through writing, I explored Circe's backstory to find out what experiences might have shaped her worldview and desire for power and fame. In Greek myth, most of the monsters are female. In retelling the story through Circe's perspective, I hope to question whether

Circe's traits of ambition, knowledge and seduction – traditionally male characteristics – are monstrous at all.

ABOUT ELISE ROBERTSON

Elise Robertson is a writer who specialises in fantasy and science fiction for children, young adults and adults. Her interests in myth, fairy tales and history influence her creative writing. She is currently working on several short stories and a first novel.

DOTTIE CALLS THE INSPECTOR

―――∽―――

ROSALIE HORNER

Dottie wakes with a start. She's back at the big house, haunted by that terrible dream again. This time she'll do something about it. Dressing in haste, she goes downstairs to telephone the police station and tell them what she knows about her dear Becca's death.

Later that day, the bell at the front door of *Becca's Bakery* rings. It's early closing in Holywell, so Dottie knows it won't be a customer. Standing on the doorstep is a large man in his fifties; he wears a dark grey suit of prewar vintage. She's pleased to see the Inspector himself. As he steps inside, his presence reassures Dottie; instinctively she knows she can trust this man, she can tell him the truth about what happened at the big house all those years ago. She's waited a decade for this; to put things right for her darling Becca.

As they walk across the flagstones of the shop, once the front room of her modest Welsh cottage, Dottie clutches her arms, rubbing them hard. It's chilly today, she thinks, leading the

Inspector through to the snug and directing him to a blue velvet armchair by the big open hearth, already laid for the evening. He sits down. Perhaps she should light the fire. She has one most nights, always making sure she throws the lighted match into the fireplace. She doesn't want any accidents here.

Dottie feels in the pockets of her cardigan for some matches and kneels on the soft mat to light the kindling. The flames leap up. She shivers and stands. Who walked over her grave?

"A cup of tea and a Becca's Bun, Inspector?"

The man shakes his head, stretching out his hands towards the now blazing fire.

Every evening Dottie comes into this little room to think her thoughts. She likes to sip her Laphroaig single malt before the warming fire; sometimes she even talks to herself. She catches sight of herself in the mirror over the mantelpiece; these days she'd be described as statuesque rather than tall and gaunt. Her hair is silver-grey and short, softening her prominent cheekbones. In the past, people said that these, and her deep-set eyes, made her face look like a skull. Not anymore, she thinks, smiling at herself with satisfaction, her face is rounded and her cheeks pink from the bracing sea air.

Dottie settles into her favourite armchair, a wingback in faded floral linen. She takes a deep breath. "I want to report a crime, one committed just before the war."

The Inspector half turns from the fire, frowning at Dottie.

"A murder for which no-one has ever been charged," she continues. "A murder for which someone should hang!"

Dottie has his full attention.

"I'll tell you our story, Inspector, then you will understand."

She crosses one ankle over the other and pushes a fallen strand of hair behind her ear.

"I was born in Charters Towers, Queensland in 1895. The town was booming in the Gold Rush. If the streets weren't paved with gold, it lay just beneath our feet waiting to be dug up, and there were plenty of diggers. Not that my father, Colonel Gerald Anderson, was one of them. No, he was there to look after the money swirling around. He loved getting his hands on all that cash. A florid-faced, portly man, he'd come to Queensland from England – Surrey to be exact – as the manager of the bank. My parents had been married for ten years and had come to terms with their childlessness. Australia was a fresh start for them, so my arrival came as a great shock. Father said my mother did her best to cope, but evidently I brought out all the misery in the world for her and she ended her days in the Charters Towers District Hospital, six months after I was born. As a consequence, I was immediately put to the local wet nurse, Nellie Furniss, who lived on the wrong side of town with her miner husband and five children. I spent nearly two years with this kind inadequate soul and, according to the town gossips, my father never called to see me once in that time."

The Inspector tuts quietly to himself. Reassured, Dottie resumes her story.

"Then one day, just before my second birthday, a coarse, disagreeable woman called Mrs Godber arrived at the Furniss's with a letter from my father, which stated she'd been appointed nanny to Dorothy Anderson, the daughter of the bank manager. She was to be my mother-substitute, responsible for rearing me, and she took me to live with my father.

"Mrs Godber might have called herself a nanny on paper, but in reality she was a tyrant. She never showed me the slightest love or kindness, preferring to cuff me rather than kiss me. My childhood became a misery. My father never tired of telling me that, after I arrived, everything went wrong for our family. I cannot remember one day when I was happy in their company. Father was selfish and pampered; he hardly gave me a second glance. I would see him briefly in the morning before he went to his office, and in the evening Mrs Godber would take me downstairs to say good night to him in his study. Before I went in to my father, she'd pinch my wrist hard, making me cry out and say, 'Make sure you kiss 'im and say you love 'im. I don't want 'im thinkin' I don't bring you up proper.'

"The most time I spent with my father was on Sundays when we went to St. Columba's Roman Catholic Church, down the road from the bank in Gill Street. In that blistering heat, Mrs Godber would dress me up in a frilly bonnet and lacy white dress with layers of petticoats like a doll. If I went out to play in our yard before church and fell over in the red dust or the mud – depending on the season – Mrs Godber would beat me with a horrible leather strap, and scream at me saying I was the Devil's child. She put the fear of God into me. When I was in church, I thought we'd be struck by lightning, die and go to Hell, and it'd be all my fault."

The Inspector shakes his head slowly from side to side, and Dottie feels he is sympathetic to her story.

"By the time I was sixteen, I was helping in the local kindergarten in Charters Towers. I loved being with the little ones. For the first time in my life I felt love for others, and my love was returned by the dear children who'd hug me whenever I came into the room. That's when I started to enjoy baking." Dottie smiles at the memory. "I'd make the children all kinds of biscuits, and a cake when it was their birthday. I've never lost my touch. That's why *Becca's Bakery* is such a success. Everyone adores my pies and pastries because they're baked with love."

The Inspector grins at Dottie and folds his arms over his chest.

"One day, a little girl of six was brought into the nursery by her aunt. She had long dark hair and her eyes were the colour of violets. She was shy and sad, and I could feel her misery at a glance; I felt I was looking at myself. I wanted to love her and take care of her. I understood her. Becca was motherless, like me, and she made what remained of my youth bearable.

"Becca's drunken father died when she was twelve, and my father agreed she could come and live with us. He made an arrangement with her aunt, who had six children of her own and couldn't look after Becca. Mrs Godber had long since gone and my father thought Becca would be company for me, but mainly an extra pair of hands to do the housework.

"Little did he know he'd done me the greatest favour of my

life. I was twenty-two and by then my father's housekeeper, responsible for cooking all the meals. Once Becca joined us, I kept the place spick and span so it would be perfect for her. Oh, what a beauty she was, even so young. Whenever we went out, men'd whistle at her. She'd smile and giggle, knowing the power she had.

Dottie chuckles to herself.

"Suddenly life became worth living. Becca and I had the house to ourselves every evening after dinner when my father went to his club to play cards. He wouldn't get home till midnight, so we could do as we wanted together in those precious hours.

"Six years later, I woke to a loud banging on our front door. A policeman stood there. He asked my name and, when I told him, he said my father was dead. He'd hanged himself in the bank, unable to face his enormous gambling debts."

The Inspector reaches out his hand as if to comfort Dottie but then withdraws it.

"There was no money left but my mother, knowing of my father's gambling habits, had established a trust for me when I was born. There was two thousand pounds in it, a fortune in those days.

"Becca and I couldn't believe it. 'We've got the world at our feet,' Becca said to me. 'Let's go and explore.' I would've followed her anywhere. I didn't have to be asked twice, and we caught the next boat from Brisbane to England. What fun we had. There were so many parties in London. We decided to say I was Becca's guardian, adding 'Mrs' to my name for respectability.

"We both had relatives in England and they embraced us as long-lost family, mainly because they were enchanted by darling Becca, no-one more so than my handsome cousin Charlie. He took her everywhere, even to Queen Charlotte's Ball at Buckingham Palace where she made her debut into London society, presented to King George the Fifth, no less."

The Inspector's head begins to droop forward.

"Can I get you a single malt, Inspector?" Dottie asks quickly, fearing the Inspector is losing interest, nodding off in the warmth of the fire.

He indicates 'no' with a slight wave of his hand and rests his head on the back of the chair.

Dottie must get to the nub of her story.

"Becca met the Master, as she liked to call him, at a soiree in Mayfair. Like Charlie, he was besotted with her; but unlike Charlie, he had money, and lots of it, and a beautiful house in the country full of old master paintings and precious objets d'art. In no time they were married and I was installed as their housekeeper. What neither of us realised was that, despite his charm, the Master was a cold, cruel man. He wanted to control Becca but her spirit was too strong for him. Gradually he grew to hate her for that."

The Inspector leans forward, looking intently at Dottie.

"I'd hear him shrieking at her when their guests left. 'You know nothing, you stupid, ignorant colonial!' He was constantly undermining her, trying to make her doubt herself. If she forgot anything, he'd grab her arm and whisper, 'You're losing your mind, my dear. You can't remember, can you?' Then he'd laugh and stride out of the room, slamming the door. She wouldn't see him for days. When he'd return, it was all smiles and sweet words and expensive gifts. I tried to warn Becca but she'd just laugh and say, 'He doesn't mean it. He's always so sorry, poor lamb. He's got a bit of a temper but nothing I can't handle.' She was always so sure of herself."

Gazing into the fire, the Inspector seems lost in thought. Dottie also stares into the hearth, but instead of seeing glowing red caverns, she sees cold underwater caves where the body of the woman she loved lay amongst the rotting planks of her little boat. Turning from the fire to the Inspector, Dottie is more resolved than ever that the truth be known.

"Becca's mistake was believing that man," she continues forcefully. "Over the years, his behaviour became more and more manipulative, and violent. In the end, she begged for a divorce, but he wouldn't hear of it. He wasn't going to have his marriage to the most beautiful woman in London society called a failure. She was so unhappy. I didn't know what to do. I suggested she contact Charlie, hoping he'd stand up to the Master on her behalf." She sighs. "He tried, but the Master just laughed, saying he'd take a shot at him if he ever trespassed his property again."

Dottie fixes her sad gaze on the Inspector. "And then it happened." Dottie's heart is racing and she pauses, taking a deep breath to calm herself so she can continue.

The Inspector straightens in his chair and stares at her.

"Becca and the Master had a violent argument and she rushed

off to her little shack, down by the water where they had a private mooring. It was her bolthole, full of her books, a comfy sofa and a couple of easy chairs. I saw him go after her and I followed them, fearing for Becca's safety. I knew the way, through the woods and down to the shore. Becca and I often went there when we wanted to be alone together."

Dottie clutches her hands in her lap, squeezing them tightly.

"But I was too late. I heard Becca laugh, then a shot. That terrible sound." Dottie covers her ears and sobs, her shoulders shaking. "I'll never forgive myself."

The Inspector's mouth is a thin line as he waits for her to gain her composure.

After some minutes, Dottie raises her chin, looking almost regal, her eyes glittering with emotion. "I saw that man drag my darling Becca's body into her little boat, smash holes in its planking, push it into the water and watch it sink beneath the waves. Then the bastard returned to the house as if nothing had happened and reported her missing." She flops back in her chair, spent.

In an eerie voice, the Inspector speaks for the first time. "Why didn't you report it?"

"I was afraid. I needed time to think, that's why I stayed on as housekeeper. I had to be careful accusing a powerful man like the Master; a man who could murder his own wife then play the grieving widower before picking up another unsuspecting orphan. That all changed when Becca's body was found with the gunshot wound. Charlie and I were sure that brute would be charged with murder, but he was clever. He was determined to prove that Becca had killed herself and, knowing she'd had a miscarriage, he got her local doctor to swear on oath that she shot herself while the balance of her mind was disturbed."

The Inspector wipes his hand over his brow.

"The Master had what he wanted – the perfect reason for Becca to kill herself. Becca suicide, never! Naturally, all the local bigwigs were only too ready to believe the wretch, anything to gain his favour and remain in his good books. But I knew the truth and I vowed one day I'd expose that man for what he is, a murderer who shot his wife in cold blood."

Dottie gets to her feet and pokes angrily at the glowing logs, turning them over to create more heat.

"Unbeknown to me, Charlie took matters into his own hands. When he picked me up at the lodge gates I smelt petrol on him, but I didn't ask any questions. I wanted to get as far away as possible from that terrible house. Charlie suggested North Wales. 'They'll never find you there, Wales is far too working class for the Master,' he sneered. Something in his voice made me turn and I saw what was once one of the most beautiful stately homes in England burst into flames, and Charlie's eyes shining in triumph."

The fire in the hearth is dying. Dottie takes a large log from the basket by the fireplace and throws it on to the glowing embers; the sparks fly out like tiny meteors.

She looks around the room. "Becca left me all she had. I owe my home and everything I possess to her. I named *Becca's Bakery* in her honour, of course. She's with me forever, but I've never had peace of mind." She sits down and wipes her eyes. "I *had* to clear Becca's name and I've done that now, Inspector."

Dottie remains silent for some minutes. "We both know he'll never be charged, don't we, Inspector? The courts can't get him while he remains outside the jurisdiction of our law." She gives a bitter laugh. "It's rather funny really, he's condemned himself to exile, to the life of a lost soul, unable to return home to the place he loves more than anything in the world."

The Inspector stands up. "You're quite right, Mrs Anderson. That is the way of things, I'm afraid. I'll see myself out." He leaves the room and Dottie hears the front door shut.

She looks across at the empty blue velvet chair and smiles. "I think it's time for that whisky."

ABOUT 'DOTTIE CALLS THE INSPECTOR'

My 'villain' is the archetypal sinister housekeeper, always written as interfering in the affairs of her mistress and master. But what if that housekeeper was really the dear friend of the mistress, and the true villain was her abusive husband? I was inspired to create Mrs Anderson after reading about Mrs. Danvers, the housekeeper obsessed with the late Rebecca de Winter in Daphne du Maurier's classic psychological thriller, *Rebecca*, published in 1938. I also found inspiration in J.B. Priestley's famous play *An Inspector Calls* where the audience is left wondering whether the Inspector actually visited at all, or whether it was the characters' own guilt that prompted their confession, and that the Inspector was a figment of their imagination. You must decide whether my strange Inspector who calls on Dottie is real or not!

ABOUT ROSALIE HORNER

Rosalie Horner is the author of two non-fiction books published in the UK, *Inside BBC Television* (Webb & Bower) and *Great TV Entertainment* (Century Benham). She was a Fleet Street journalist for thirty years; firstly, on the Daily Express as a gossip columnist, television and theatre reviewer, then freelance for most of Fleet Street. She has written for the magazines *Radio Times*, *Saga* and *Woman's Own*, and been a panellist on TV shows *New Faces*, *Celebrity Squares*, *Telly Addicts* and *Tell the Truth*. She was Chair of the Broadcasting Press Guild for two years, in a writing group in London, and has done various writing courses there and abroad. Rosalie is an Australian who lived in London for many years and returned to Sydney in 2018.

BOTOX AND BATS

―――――⌇―――――

MEGAN ROHLEDER

The clinic smelt of cleaning fluid and antibacterial lotion. Ella took a deep breath, enjoying the smell of sterility. It was her third favourite, losing out only to petrol stations and smoke. The nurse leaned in closer as she stretched the skin to the right of Ella's eye tighter. She had such young blemish-free skin and glossy blonde hair. Ella clutched the seat tightly, eyeing the white of her knuckles. What else could she do to resist the urge to cut the nurse's hair off and take it from her as a wig – paying meagrely for it of course? Ella diverted her eyes from the scissors on the side trolley, taking in the rising damp, which made the paint peel off the walls. What was it her therapist had said? Count to ten to control your urges and don't compare your current circumstances to rose-tinted views of the past. One, two, three…

"You'll feel a sharp pain, but it won't last long. Stop me any time if it gets too much." The nurse's voice was meek like a dying mouse, and her fingers shook as she put the needle to Ella's face.

"I don't bite, despite what you might have heard," Ella cackled.

"Of course not." Now the nurse's hands trembled violently. "Please keep your head still." She inserted the point.

Ella fixated again on the golden hair that fell softly to frame the nurse's face and then on her own white knuckles. Four, five, six. She stopped counting and let out a sigh as the transparent liquid filled her veins. Honey for her soul. She took a deep breath in and held it, not wanting the other-worldly feeling to end.

"Well, that didn't hurt as much as the injections I have every ten years to prolong my life!" Ella chuckled. "Each one makes me twenty years younger. Did I tell you about those? I presume you've not heard of them." She glanced at the mould gathering in the corners of the room and the stained blinds. "My last beauty clinic offered them, but this isn't quite the same clientele… and, well, they are quite expensive. I've got another one coming up, though." She flicked her black Tibetan sand fox stole off her right shoulder, then twisted her wrist to admire her pearl bracelet catching the light.

"It takes time for the Botox to settle." The nurse pressed and held the needle point in place with her bare fingers, her hands violently shaking.

"Save your words on me, darling. I've spent more on Tox than your parents did paying off their mortgage." Ella smirked.

The girl pulled the needle free. Ella felt another intense pain, then a slow drip down her cheek. Blood? She looked at the tears welling in the young girl's eyes. What a wimp!

The girl stood up and walked to the pedal bin, pressing the pedal with her pink ballet pump, and discarding the needle while avoiding Ella's eyes. The sound of it hitting the base of the bin cut through the awkward silence between them. God knows what, if any, Botox had made it into her face.

"You can get up after ten minutes have passed."

Ella tutted, before immediately rising from the treatment chair, picking up her keys and bags, and making her way to the door.

The young girl hovered behind her. "If you, erm, if you insist on leaving, we take payment over here, please." She pointed at the white reception desk, adorned with fake flowers and a bowl of Mentos. The lit candle caught her attention – how she loved fire and a naked flame. Such danger!

"Didn't they tell you? I never pay, just add it to my account, darling. Laters, sweetie." She swung the door open, let it slam behind her, then slumped against it. How long could she keep everything going, while they had no money and no house of their own? She took her phone from her pocket and flicked on Instagram.

Holy dachshunds! Hadn't she asked Frank, her inept husband, to put an engaging post up while she was out? She tutted at the dull picture of a dog in a plastic rain jacket. Their business simply had to do better than that – they'd made no sales in the last two months! So what if their previous line of fashion furs had been cancelled by online do-gooders – dogs were cuisine in some countries! Everyone deserved a second chance.

That was it, she needed to do something herself.

She typed a message to her caretaker, Henry.

How long did you say it would take for us to get squatter's rights in the mansion?

She stared at the screen and winced as the Botox moved under her skin, like small worms finding room for air. Ha, they wouldn't find much oxygen in her body! She cackled again before steadying her eyes and mind. Seven, eight, nine... That's right, she needed to be more forceful. She couldn't bear to let people know she and her husband were squatting. She'd rather sleep in the raincoat storage shed than a bedsit. She messaged Henry again:

Fake the papers or something, just see to it that we can stay there for the foreseeable. Also, sack our social media marketing team – they and Frank are useless. Ta-ta. E.

Heat rose from the tarmac as she strode along the street. Despite the warm London summer, she shivered, and pulled her fur stole tighter round her neck and took her lambswool jumper from her handbag.

A man walked by, struggling with three dogs on leads. He moved into a sideways shuffle as he passed her and kept his head down. There was a thud as one of the stubby black dogs suddenly scurried from him, making him stumble onto his hands and knees.

"Watch it!" She hissed. "Animals can cause all sorts of accidents. You could have damaged my Birkin!" Well, fake Birkin, but no one knew that.

The man dusted himself off. He had a familiar face –
that pointed nose and those golden ringlets... and the dogs,
dachshunds.

Had the Botox got to her? Why hadn't she noticed those first?

"Storm! What's gotten into you?" He patted the largest of the
tiny dogs and glanced up at Ella. His eyebrows raised and his lips
quivered. "He, erm, doesn't normally react like that." He started
walking in the opposite direction.

Ella ran after him, the speed of her jog slightly warming her
face. She grabbed his shoulder. "You're a Meek, aren't you? I
know your mother." Mrs Meek had been one of the lead activists
who shut down their fur business. She looked the man up and
down.

"She's been dead a few years now." He kept his eyes on his
feet.

One of the smaller dachshunds came up and licked Ella's
leg. She jumped at the physical contact. He had a cute pixie face
and a vibrant pink tongue. Still, a pain like a furrier stripping her
carcass with a knife seared through the back of her head. She
pressed her finger against it. Had the injection impacted her?
No, she had Botox all the time. She looked again at the dog, who
now rested at her feet, its big dark eyes gazing innocently at her.
She actually quite liked him.

Frank ran to the en suite and splashed more ice-cold water on the already saturated flannel. "It's unlike you to be this hot, Ella. I didn't think your body was capable of such warmt–"

"It was that deplorable new Botox nurse. It's all your fault. If you'd shifted more of those raincoats, I could afford to go to decent places," she snarled.

Frank pressed the flannel on her forehead, at arm's length.

"Get me my last fur coats from the cupboard," she growled.

"I don't think that's the best idea… you have quite a fever already."

"I don't want to wear them, you idiot. We need to sell some!" She hobbled towards the wardrobe, but her head started spinning, so she stopped and sat on the edge of the bed.

Frank scrambled off to what had once been an extensive walk-in wardrobe. There was the sound of coat hangers being flung to the ground and the scraping of others moving along the rails. "Erm, you're not going to like this, Ella. There are quite a lot of marks…"

The furious sound of scraping mixed with Frank's panting.

"What's going on?" Ella lifted herself from the bed to see Frank on his knees, scrubbing a fur coat with his nails. Ella waved her bony fists in the air.

"What are those yellow marks? I've been saving these coats for years!" She hurried forward to grab the matted mess of material, kissed it and wailed. "Henry!"

Heavy footsteps sped up the stairs and Henry rushed in, panting.

"What's happened to my fur?"

"I told you there was an influx of rodents, rats, bats, you name it. This place fell into disrepair when the Russians left… we can't apply for pest control as we don't have legal ownership, ma'am."

Ella picked up a mop of black fur, saturated in yellow liquid and shook it in Frank's face. "Urgh, piss! Frank, look what you've done to us. You can't even keep a roof over your wife's head."

"I think it might be the bats that got through in the storm the other night." Henry choked.

"Out! Just go Henry, you've done enough. Don't expect to come back tomorrow!"

"What about all the arrears?" He held his palm to his head. "You haven't paid me in six months, and you promised you'd make it worth my while. I even found you this place."

"Well, you've got Frank to thank for that. All his idea, those plastic bloody raincoats. He hasn't sold one in two months!" she yelled.

"Ella, you've lost it," Frank mumbled. "It's not my fault the raincoats aren't selling. You priced them way too high, like we are some fancy goods company or something."

She started pelting Frank and Henry with fake designer shoes.

"Frank's got a point, Ella." Henry yelped as a shoe hit him in the arm. "Fur just ain't 'in' no more, no matter what the animal. This day and age it's all 'ship it in and sell it cheap'." Henry managed to duck before Ella hurled another shoe and he ran out the bedroom door.

The slam of the door reverberated through Ella. She caught her reflection in the mirror. No makeup and all exposed. What was that on her cheek? She walked closer to the mirror and saw a large red spot on her cheek, surrounded by numerous wrinkles. There was another circle down her neck. She took off her dress, turned and counted four cruddy circles on her back. Varicose veins snaked up a leg. Is this what she paid all that money for every ten years, to extend her life to look this way? Surely she hadn't looked this bad yesterday...

Wait! That Botox nurse must have injected her with aging fluid, rather than Botox! Ella fell to her hands and knees. What was she doing? Is this all her one precious life would come to, the life she worked so hard to prolong? No business? No money? No marriage? And someone out there hated her so much, they'd pay a nurse to inject her with something so evil? Come to think of it, she had so many enemies now, she couldn't possibly pick who had done it!

She walked over to the pile of rodent urine-stained fur coats and picked them up one by one. Each brought a memory of an occasion, but all the feelings attached to those memories seemed to have been stripped away. She remembered wearing one to show she was a glamorous heiress, but couldn't recall the fun she had there. The black and brown striped fur coat with pearls sewn in caught her eye. She had worn that to Mrs Meek's dinner party, when she and the activist had been trying to come to some arrangement over the fashion furs. How many years ago now? Ella didn't want to know. And the Meek son she had bumped into on the street – how old was he now? His dogs were cute. She didn't even have a child or a pet.

Ella took a deep inhale of her e-cigarette and held her breath for as long as possible. There was something about depriving her brain of oxygen that still gave her a thrill. She turned to Henry.

"When did you say the first shipment of bats was coming from Chonasia?"

"I told you, Ella, we can have 'em here in a couple of days, but I told ya my mate Joe says they've all got that illness now. You know, the new mad cow disease or whatever they wanna call it."

"Sod those illnesses. It's better than dog fur. I'm reformed, Henry." She threw her head back with a cackle before taking another drag on her e-cigarette.

"That's not how the authorities see it. You got to be careful transporting live animals."

She sashayed over to Henry, her long black dress sweeping the floor. She put her face close to his. "Then have them killed there and brought over. If we can say they're locally made, it'll add to their value; but at this stage, do whatever needs doing!"

"But Ella, it's a criminal…"

"I'll consider it done." She stubbed her e-cigarette on the ashtray, momentarily forgetting it wasn't the real thing. "While you're at it, order me some more cigarette pipes. Not these modern imitations. I'm sick of them."

Ella adjusted her fur dressing gown. It felt itchy. She twitched and moved her neck from side to side as she stretched her slender and increasingly aching body in bed. Needing a distraction, she leant over to her bedside table and picked up the newspaper and coffee Henry had left, as he always did. Frank pulled the covers over him. She yanked them off and kicked his leg.

"Frank, you need to be up and working. These bat fur coats won't make or sell themselves."

Frank jumped up and into the en suite, locking the door behind him.

Ella relaxed back on the silk cushion and took a sip of coffee before reading the front page:

Dogs dying, as experts fear another disease brought in by bats.

She spat her coffee out, flinching as she scalded her hand, before continuing to read.

'Several dogs have been taken ill, driven by a new virus, Concocta C, believed to have been imported from Chonasian bats… Mr Meek, whose dachshunds died two days ago as a result of the illness, commented, 'devastated is the word, we have bred these dogs as a family for years and never have we seen them die so quickly.'

She jumped up and rattled the en suite door. How could this have happened? She hated to think of that gorgeous dog dying from a stupid virus, its cute pixie face drooping with sickness, its big dark eyes all sad.

"Frank! Burn the bat fur! Now."

The en suite door slowly unlatched.

Ella barged in.

Frank was hovering over the toilet seat, sweat pooling on his forehead. "What? Have you finally gone mad?"

She shoved the newspaper in his face. "Read this. We've got no choice, Frank."

She hitched her muted red tulle nightdress into her knickers and ran downstairs. Piles of black, brown, and speckled bat fur stood out against the marble floor in the lounge. She gathered a pile in her hands and started shunting them into the middle of the room, kicking any straggly bits as she dropped them on the floor. The Russians who had left the place deserted had taken half the furniture with them, giving her room to spread out the furs.

"Frank!" Ella screamed up the stairs. "Where are the matches?"

Frank's footsteps clomped loudly as he ran downstairs. "You said you wanted to get rid of all the matches in the house, as part of your last round of therapy. I don't know if I'm coming or going. Why have you moved all these to the middle of the floor?" His voice was shaking.

"Didn't you read the paper!" she shrieked.

Frank covered his ears and looked at the ground.

Ella swallowed, swirled the remaining saliva round in her very dry mouth and puffed out her skirt. "Compose yourself, Ella," she muttered to herself. "You've got no time for this." She walked over to Frank. "The newspaper said that animals are dying from an imported bat disease. We've got to destroy the evidence."

"I've got a lighter in the kitchen, but you'll burn the house down." His voice was hoarse.

"It's not ours anyway." Ella hurried into the kitchen.

"But what about the neighbours?"

He had a point. "You run and tell them there's a fire. I'll get the lighter." Ella yanked open the kitchen drawers one at a time, spilling contents to the floor. Finally, the lighter fell out, and she grabbed it before running back to the lounge. Electricity pulsed through her body as she flicked the lighter on and fixated on the glare. She'd normally be mesmerised, even trance-like, at the sight of a flame, but she felt nothing except fear. Fear of the unknown and what was about to happen.

She slapped her face and threw the lighter on the pile of bat furs. There was a small sizzling sound, like someone putting a cigarette out, then nothing. The flame fizzled out. Why wouldn't it catch light? Were all these furs fake, synthetic? Ella glared at the pile like it was an adequate summary of her life.

Sirens wailed in the distance.

"Oh no!" Her throat constricted as the sirens approached.

She had to go. She grabbed a coat and ran to the door, pushing open the heavy door, before tripping over and falling forward as her hands were pulled and tightened behind her back. Someone was grabbing her. Kidnapping her?

"Frank! Frank!" she yelled, turning her head.

Two men dressed in heavy armour and black uniforms were holding her down. "Ella Ashlyn we are arresting you on suspicion of smuggling illegal disease-bearing animals into the country."

She yanked at the handcuffs to see if she could loosen them, but the metal clasps didn't shift. The officers pulled her to her feet and escorted her to their waiting police car. The grounds were swarming with officers in HazMat suits, and paparazzi yelled at her from the front gates, shouting something about 'the downfall of the dame of doom'. How on this earth had any of them known?

She caught sight of Mr Meek on the other side of the road, holding two dachshunds. Had he done this?

The prison church was quiet and still for a spring evening. It had been three years since Ella's incarceration, so three years since Ella had first attended and spoken to the prison chaplain about her woes and guilt and regrets. At first it was just to try and get early release, but then because… why did she still come?

The chaplain lowered his glasses onto the bridge of his nose. He didn't look directly at her, just continued staring at a single candle flickering next to the wooden cross in front of him. Ella found the light of the candle soothing and calming, unlike the buzz she would normally get from being exposed to fire and its danger. That bloody therapist she'd spent an arm and a leg on these past few years would be proud!

Finally, the chaplain turned to face her. His eyes were warm and sparkled in the candle-lit prison chapel.

"So let me get this straight, you can't get your injection to keep prolonging your life and you can't get Botox in here, so you believe you will shortly die?"

Putting it like that, it sounded laughable. She straightened herself in her seat. "I do, and I'm fine with that. It won't happen straight away, but I am now very old. And I've had time to think in here. To make real friends. I don't want my old life anymore. The fact that I clearly brought so much pain to all those darling creatures."

"And their owners."

"Sure, sure." She dismissed the idea with a flick of her hand. "Anyway darling," Ella was breathless, but lowered her voice, so it was barely audible. "Since reflecting in here, I think I'd like to grow old gracefully now. I think there's something in it." A book maybe, glitzy enough to be sold to the rich and famous…

"Talking of reflection, we received a letter from a Mr Meek. Allow me to read the important part. 'Ella, you might not know this, but my mum actually used to admire you, living your crazy executive life, rolling in money and the finer things, while she was left picking up dog poo. I never understood why, given you were simply evil, and she was such a good person, campaigning for animal rights the way she did. She hated having to speak out against your dog fur business. But what choice did she have? She lived for her dogs, and for her dog retreat. We know it was you who burnt it down. She refused to take action of course, so I decided you needed a taste of your own medicine and hired the Botox nurse to inject you with aging fluid. I also got a private detective to look at your business activities, and pass that information on to the police. Hopefully, Mother can now rest in peace, and you've learnt a lesson. And I truly hope you have.' What do you think of that, Ella?" the chaplain asked.

Ella felt herself getting warm, despite the cold plastic chairs and cold concrete walls. She jumped up from her seat and started pacing. Some people were so stupid. To think they knew her enough to judge. What did they know? All she'd ever done was try her best. It wasn't her fault her parents had died when she was young and left her scrabbling for money.

Ella took a breath and started counting. One, two, three…

At least she didn't have to worry about money anymore – all her accommodation, food and toiletries were free and always would be now. That Mr Meek could go…

Four, five, six…

No one was 'simply evil', that was an exaggeration, and a mean one at that. Mr Meek was completely wrong, and she would prove it to him. All she had to do was a nice deed for others, and make sure he knew about it. But what could she do, surrounded by hundreds of dowdy women who clearly had lost all hope of ever looking remotely decent – as evident in the group of inmates shuffling past outside the chaplain's window. Ugly navy jumpsuits, tattered hems, and missing buttons, covered in stains. Unkempt hair. Slouched postures. No self-worth or pride or…

Seven, eight, nine…

Unless that was the answer. Unless she could help them, all of them.

Ten…

"Do you think I could get a sewing machine?" she asked the chaplain with a soft confidence. "I would like to start giving some of the other women here sewing classes, you know, so they can work towards something for themselves. For the entire prison perhaps?"

"That could be arranged." The chaplain scribbled in his notebook.

Ella snatched it from him.

He jumped and skidded back into his chair.

"Sorry, I didn't mean to frighten you. I'm just very passionate about my work." She gave him an apologetic smile. At least, she hoped it was.

"The guards warned me to be extra careful, you know."

Ella chuckled, then concentrated on writing in his notebook. He would need to get a lot of materials, but he was sure to find donations – especially with a little advertising. Once all her ideas were down, she handed the notebook back.

He read it slowly. "'Local Women's Prison Announce New Bespoke Designer Wear On Sale Now – 'Creations by Ella'. Donate now to support local!' Ella," the chaplain stumbled, "this is…"

"An amazing idea, yes, I know. I've learnt, being in here, it's just the simple things, not money, that are truly satisfying. I'm going to write a self-help book too. You know, 'Growing old gracefully and how to live a satisfying life' or maybe even 'How I started a fashion label in prison'."

He smiled briefly, then studied her other notes, flipping through the pages.

As she waited, she caught sight of the picture on his desk – of his children and presumably a family cat. If all else failed, perhaps she could get Henry to smuggle in some Persian cat fur?

ABOUT 'BOTOX AND BATS'

This story explores the archetype of a business villain who is focused on maximising profit for personal financial reward, with zero concern for anyone or anything else. I took inspiration from several literary villains, including the insatiable businessman Jordan Belfort from *The Wolf of Wall Street* and the charismatic bully Cruella de Ville from *101 Dalmatians*. It tells the story of how Ella attempts to live a more moral life and become less selfish. Ashamed of killing dogs for fur, she turns to bats, leading to her imprisonment for bringing a new virus into the country.

ABOUT MEGAN ROHLEDER

Megan Rohleder is an author who lives in Fairlight on the Northern Beaches. She has a Bachelor and Master of Arts from Oxford University. Her first novel, *Trading Up*, is about to be published.

THREE HEARTS

————ᴏᴠᴏ————

SONIA ZADRO

"Through my longing I came to know her hearts; her first contained her mischief, her second her laughter, and her third her tenderness. I loved them all, but she gave not one to me."

Towering waves, black and omnipotent, pounded and thrashed in the lightning of the midnight storm, while Kertarla's eight thick monstrous tentacles flailed in fury. Octopus Queen of the oceanic underworld, Kertarla was at breaking point. She was consumed by her rage at the Sea King Nereus, by her rage at Zeus, by her rage at Jupiter and all the Gods, including Klothos the God of fate; but above all she was enraged at herself. Because for all her power and magic, she could not make Prince Jarek of Averna, love her.

In fact, Jarek hadn't even given Kertarla a second glance. Instead, Kertarla thought to herself, he'd pathetically pined after that spoilt skinny blonde, Talassa, the ninth of King Nereus' twelve daughters. Kertarla emphatically refused to accept this. In the name of Zeus and all the Gods, when did curves – good solid voluptuous curves – go out of fashion? Damn it, if she couldn't fill her own cup of love, then she would damn well fill her cup of power – a cup, Kertarla noticed, that felt terribly satisfying to fill, though rather bottomless.

And so she thrashed her muscled tentacles, and they soared and glistened in the lightning as the storm raged. Yes, the Gods had chosen to meet her now in this place of fury – condemning her for her wayward behaviour. So what if they didn't approve of her capturing Talassa and sequestering her away while Kertarla magically disguised herself in an attempt to win the Prince's heart? She didn't damn well need their stupid approval anyway. She was owed this. Her life had been one of endless relentless disappointment; in love, in friendship, not to mention all the abuse she had to put up with growing up for being shy, fat, and musically inept. Some people were simply born tone deaf with a bad metabolism. She shouldn't have to cop more bad luck on top of all that. No, she shouldn't, and so she'd made her own luck in life and found her calling – to pluck the merfolk from their insignificant little lives and steal their energy to feed her magic.

So as the waves pounded out their wrath, the more terrified Talassa became; and the greater her terror, the more merfolk fear Kertala absorbed, fuelling her with magic and power, until she grew larger and larger, her eyes gleaming bright and yellow, brimming with hate and wrath. It was all so wonderful and delicious. Licking her thick orange lips in pleasure, Queen Kertala released a mighty squeal of delight as she grasped the mermaid Talassa in one of her thick tentacles.

Talassa screamed in terror as Kertarla's laugh tumbled over the turbulent waters. For the first time in her life, Kertarla felt truly powerful, in control and safe, and she felt it all deep within her troubled mixed-up soul. She paused a moment to let this sink in and smiled a satisfied smile. How far she had come from that messed-up heartbroken teenager.

Abruptly her smile vanished, and a scream pierced the storm; a scream so intense, so agonised, that by the time Kertarla realised it was her own, she was already sinking below the ocean's surface. Prince Jarek steered the spar protruding from the lower side of his Avernian warship directly through Kertarla's heart. In mere moments, her monstrous form shrank to its former size. Kertarla wailed in pain as she sank, deeper and deeper, to the vast depths of the dark ocean floor.

Kertarla lay there, in the dark, for hours, and were it not for the saving grace of her three hearts, she would have died. For as luck would have it, all giant Pacific octopus', including herself, have three hearts – one to circulate blood through their enormous bodies, and two other hearts to pump blood past the gills to pick up oxygen. It was one of these latter two hearts that the warship's spar had pierced on this stormy night. Such an injury would have killed any other species of octopus in an instant – three hearts or not – but in this instance, fate had stepped in.

When Kertarla regained consciousness, she was so weak, she could barely move a tentacle. Slowly, she opened her eyes, now back to their original dark blue colour, and found herself staring into a pair of eyes uncannily similar to her own. She blinked and glanced around. She appeared to be in a cave of some sort, with a wide sandy bottom and sunlight filtering in through a roof opening. Other than an abundance of colourful seaweed growing along the cave's edges, all alit with the sun's dappled light, the cave was empty. No fish, no crabs, no sea urchins. They were completely alone.

The other creature, which she now realised was also a giant Pacific octopus, reached out one long tentacle and stroked one of Kertarla's thick long tentacles. "Kertarla," it whispered soothingly.

Almost identical in appearance to herself, the onlooker appeared deeply concerned, which was very strange indeed, because Kertarla had never experienced the concern of another living creature in her life. Her eyes narrowed. Kertala was not used to being touched, not ever. Abruptly, she retracted her tentacle from the creature. The movement of her still-sore body caused her to cry out in pain.

"Oh dear," the onlooker's worry lines deepened. "Oh dear, oh dear, oh dear. My sweeting, you are one messed up octopus indeed." The creature gently turned and settled some distance away.

Kertarla's deep voice came out as a gravelly whisper. "And wh… who are you?"

The octopus looked affronted. "What? Well, I'm your knight in shining armour. Who else!" He laughed. "Who am I indeed!"

Kertarla rolled her eyes and shook her foggy head. "I think we can all agree," she croaked, "that knights in shining armour and happy endings are a lot of rot." Her voice was still gravelly, but she managed to bellow out the word 'rot'. It seemed to help her find her voice again. "I am an expert in the subject," she continued, "destroying others' happy endings, that is. Do you know how many fairy tale endings I've salaciously destroyed – sucking in the joy and love of those deluded souls for my own pleasure, before throwing them back into the pit of damnation for all eternity?" She chuckled. "And then there's my own life to go by – no one can screw up as epically as me, mister... what was your name? And didn't you see what I just went through? Happy endings…" She shook her head.

The other octopus waved one tentacle dismissively. "Yes, yes, Kertarla, the evil sea queen making the merfolk of the world utterly miserable – you play the evil incarnate archetype perfectly."

"I play…" Kertarla's voice boomed – or at least it attempted to.

"Spare your voice, please. I have applied a clamp on your heart to stop the bleed – molluscs are so handy for that sort of thing – but you will be sore."

Kertarla glanced down. "A clamp?"

The mysterious octopus continued to observe her with disapproval, disappointment and… was that compassion?

Kertarla shuddered. Hatred, rage, disapproval, fear – they were all perfectly tolerable, even enjoyable to incite in others, given the power it gave her – but compassion? Ugh, she shuddered. Compassion made her want to throw up.

The creature scratched its head with one tentacle and looked at her tenderly.

"My dear Queen, I am your Uncle Orphelius."

"Uncle what? Who?"

"Orphelius, on your father's side. You won't remember, but I was with you in your younger years, particularly during your schooling. I helped advise your parents on preparing you for the throne. They certainly needed the help, as did you. But I kept my distance. I cradled you in my tentacles when you were first born." His eyes misted over for a second and he appeared to look beyond her. "My, you were a sweeting."

"An uncle?" Now she thought about it, Kertarla was starting to recognise him. There had been occasions when she returned from her schooling in her younger years, when he had been there. But he had never introduced himself and had always seemed in a rush to leave soon after she arrived home.

"Your parents forbade me from being anywhere near you back then. They didn't believe in affection. They thought it weakened the constitution. I'm sure you remember that all too well. Let's just say I kept a close watch from afar."

Kertarla frowned, clearly sceptical. "And what are you doing here now?"

"Isn't it obvious? You, my liege, are in dire need of serious guidance." The octopus moved around as he spoke with a casual air. "Guidance, which just so happens to be my specialty."

"Guidance?" Kertarla looked over at him. "Great, so you'll help me nail the tramp and ruin her little rendevous with the sea prince? Then sink my titillating tentacles into King Nereus and get his trident – it belongs in the hands of a strong deserving woman, like me, not some pathetic spineless excuse for a king!"

Uncle Orphelius eyed her sternly. "Therapy. When I said guidance, I meant more along the lines of therapy. I'm terribly good at it."

Kertarla stilled, and slowly frowned back at him.

"I will help you apologise to King Nereus, give Talassa and her prince your blessing, as her father has done, set free all the merfolk whose fearful souls you've captured, and encourage you to live a happy and peaceful life that does not involve interfering in the lives of others, or for that matter, damning the souls of any more harmless innocent merfolk for all eternity."

Kertarla stared at her uncle for several moments, speechless, then with all the flourish she could muster, she threw her head back and laughed, or rather, bellowed, so loudly her uncle had to cover his ears with two of his tentacles. When her laughter ceased, she held her belly with one tentacle and winced as she wiped tears of laughter from her eyes.

"Ouch, ow, that does hurt. Ooh, but please, I love it. So when do we start? This is going to be a hoot."

Uncle Orphelius frowned and narrowed his eyes, his colour changing from black to brown. He moved closer to Kertarla and stared her down. "We start now."

Kertarla was not intimidated. "Whoopee. So shoot, Orphy." She lowered her voice and smiled. "Watcha got? Poor fat Kertarla teased for being fat, shy and dumb at school, or is it poor little

Kertarla whose parents toughened her up by abusing her with their vicious insults and cold indifference?"

Orphelius paused and smiled back. He hesitated, then spoke. His tone was matter of fact. "Arabella Winters."

The smile fell from Kertarla's face and her colour paled to a peachy grey. For a moment she couldn't move. Eventually, she spun away from her uncle and moved to the back of the cave. There she remained silent.

"I know you loved her."

Kertarla stiffened.

After the silence had stretched for some time, her uncle continued. "Others didn't know how close you had become, how deeply you felt her affection…"

Still facing away from her uncle, Kertarla responded in a whisper. "I had never known how it felt to be loved."

"I know, my dear," he said quietly. "Your parents were not kind people. Not at all. My brother was a special kind of cruel, he held a special kind of cold indifference, and your mother… she gave a whole new meaning to the word narcissism. She didn't love you the way you deserved, Kertarla."

"The way I deserved? The way *anyone* deserved!"

"Yes, in the way anyone deserved." Uncle Orphelius inched a little closer. "And then the bullying at school. And then Arabella…"

Kertarla remembered. Still facing away, she whispered. "Only *I* really knew her – her mischief, her laughter, her… her tenderness. I didn't know how close two octopuses could be and not… you know, take it further. When I found her with *him*…" Kertarla's colour changed to a deep red, her eyes now dark with pain.

Her uncle extended a tentacle toward Kertarla. He softened his voice to a whisper. "I know, my darling girl. I know."

Kertarla stared at the tentacle her uncle had offered to her, then thrust it away as though it were poison. She moved to the far end of the cave so he wouldn't hear her crying softly to herself. "You shouldn't touch me," she snapped, trying to hide her emotions. "No one should touch my venomous skin, my poisonous blood, my evil soul."

Uncle Orphelius looked over at Kertarla with eyes full of compassion. "And now she is no longer with us, it still breaks your hearts."

Kertarla's arms flamed orange and red. She turned and bellowed at him. "Yes, I miss her, of course I miss her. But don't you see, uncle? I took her soul and I destroyed it! *I* killed her! *I* murdered her! And I've been taking souls ever since. I finally found something I'm good at." Her voice became a hiss then. "Such unforgiveable evil."

Her uncle paused and frowned. He seemed quite perplexed. He then spoke softly. "But Kertarla, you didn't kill her."

Kertarla narrowed her eyes. "What do you mean? I shook her… and shook her… she collapsed. The next day when I returned to see her, she was dead."

"Yes, but didn't you see how weak she was when you fought? What little fight she had in her."

Kertarla frowned and rubbed her head with one tentacle. "I know she was depressed. She wanted to be with that other bastard, but he wouldn't have her. She wanted him. Him, not me."

"Kertarla, Arabella had only lain her eggs three days prior. She was simply due to die, just like every other octopus of our species – four days after laying her eggs. She was due to die the very day after you saw her."

Kertarla stared at him for several moments. "She was p… pregnant?"

"I searched for you relentlessly, but you had vanished. I blamed your parents. By God, I was so furious with them. I thought you were dead. I only discovered how far you had travelled when I heard about your dealings with Prince Jarek and King Nereus."

"She was *pregnant*?"

Her uncle paused and inched slowly towards her. "Yes, your choices were bad." He nodded to himself. "And your behaviour, it wasn't good… but you were not responsible for Arabella's death."

"But, I *wanted* to hurt her; and I did hurt her." She looked up at her uncle, her eyes pleading. "I hurt her badly."

"Yes. Yes, you did. But I know your hearts, Kertarla – I've known them since you were a babe, all pure and shiny, and… well, let's just say they were terribly hurt, those hearts. The first heart did not survive your parents' neglect and cruelty, your second heart did not survive the cruelty you experienced at school, and then, and then losing your one true love, well, your third heart... it didn't stand a chance."

Kertarla sank to the floor of the cave, as though all the fight in her had left.

Her uncle continued, "I saw you with Arabella. She was your twin soul – but she couldn't see it. I know she couldn't see it."

Kertarla let out a cry, a keening wail that rang across the ocean floor. She cried for her one true unrequited love, for the absence of her parents' love, for the pain she suffered from those who bullied her at school, for the torment she had inflicted on so many souls, and for all the torment she had inflicted on herself. She moaned and sobbed out all the pain and hurt from her three hearts, until eventually, she quietened and her uncle moved closer.

He placed his eight tentacles around her exhausted body and gently held her in his tender love.

And finally, Kertarla let him.

ABOUT 'THREE HEARTS'

My story explores the archetype of the evil incarnate sea monster, who needs to heal the forces that drive their wrath. Inspired by fairy tales such as 'The Little Mermaid' by Hans Christian Andersen (1837), as well as myths and legends of Greek mythology, 'Three Hearts' is about unrequited love in its many forms and its power to destroy. It is also about the importance of vulnerability and allowing others in, as the first step to healing.

ABOUT SONIA ZADRO

Sonia Zadro is a clinical psychologist and freelance magazine writer. Her stories '52 Hertz' and 'Yenali' were selected for inclusion in the 2019 and the 2020 Manly Arts Festival's 'Art & Words Project' in the anthologies *Saltwater* and *Portrait* respectively. Her story 'Oscar' gained highly commended in the 2016 BezerkaCon competition and was published in the anthology *A Fearsome Engine* (NBWG, 2016). Her other stories, 'The Big Dipper' and 'Bachorella' were published in other NBWG anthologies.

HEZZE: THE GINGERBREAD HAG

---cvᴐ---

AVI VINCE

I released my grey hair from its tightly woven bun. It fell like brittle straw over my shoulder, scratching the thinning skin on my hands as I smoothed it down. I turned away from the musty smell of my cottage to the rare breath of fresh air spilling through the open shutters. It felt like light hadn't touched the sodden earth in months. The heavy black clouds hovered above, threatening more disaster.

The girl's squeal pierced my silent home. I peered across my struggling herbs, over the rotting wooden fence, past the flower garden their mother once kept with such pride, and saw the two children chasing each other through the sludge. Hansel seemed to pretend to run slowly, as if he was letting his little sister think she might finally be too fast for him. As Hansel came up to Gretel, he gently wrapped his arms around her, a fit of laughter enveloping them. Suddenly, their stepmother flung open the door, destroying a moment of pure childhood.

"Hansel, get your grimy hands off her." Their stepmother

stomped across the wet ground towards him and hit him twice across the head. My body jerked at the sound, which carried across the yard.

"And you." She rounded on Gretel and grabbed her by the ear, pulling her up so high she was on her tippy toes, whimpering. "Look at your dress!"

Hansel begged his stepmother to stop. He apologised, explaining they were just having fun. He pulled at her arm, despite her towering over his ten-year-old frame. In one fluid movement, the stepmother released Gretel, causing her to crumple to the ground, and back-handed Hansel across his cheek so hard he fell into the mud. They were far dirtier now than when they were playing.

"Today's chores. And tomorrow's. Then we shall see if you have time for such childish games. *And* no dinner. Maybe with grumbling stomachs, you'll learn to be more respectful."

Their concave bellies would grumble, with or without dinner. In the never-ending famine, the once beautiful plump face of their stepmother was now only a collection of pointy features. But she had always been cruel. She was so unlike their real mother, Gertrude, who Gretel never got to meet.

Every day, the smell from Gertrude's kitchen would waft into my nostrils. As I pruned and picked my herbs, my stomach would somersault with desire. In the late afternoon, Gertrude would leave her house, her arms heavy with a covered bowl and a bundle, and walk along the path that snaked around their property and into mine. "Frau Hezze," she would call out as she swung open my gate.

None of the other villagers would openly address me with such respect, instead I knew they called me a Zauberin, or sorcerer, behind my back. They would come for my potions of course, sneaking their way to me covered in hoods, as if that would mask their identity. Jasmine to fall in love, Red Clover to bear children, and more recently, my onion broth for the fluid that lay in their lungs. Once I had met their needs, they'd go back to their filthy stories about meine Liebe Otto slipping into death a few days after promising himself to me – his due for marrying a cursed woman from a cursed family.

Not Gertrude. She would patiently wait outside my door while I shuffled to greet her. There she would stand with the most fragrant of aromas seeping out of the covered bowl filled with stew. In her other hand, she would hold out the freshly baked bread wrapped in cloth. "Frau Hezze, I made too much dinner for my husband and I, please help me not waste it."

In return, I would share with her the ginger cookies I'd made from my grandmother's recipe. "Sweet and good for the digestion," I always said.

Gertrude made that walk every afternoon, regardless of the size of her growing belly. Hansel screamed from the minute he breathed the world's clean air and could only be tamed by his mother's beautiful singing, which I would listen to as I plucked the leaves and flowers that my mother and grandmother had taught me to grow. Within a few days of his birth, she resumed her walk to my home, Hansel strapped to her chest.

"You don't need to feed me, you have a baby to care for now. You must look after him. And yourself," I said.

She still came. Each and every afternoon. Hansel wobbling along on his nearly two-year-old legs. Her belly growing once more.

She left this world when her daughter entered it. There was no Gertrude to soothe the wailing baby. I fell into the same despair that had once blackened the walls when I lost meine Liebe. Was it my fault? Were the village fools right? Was this my curse? To lose those who showed me kindness. The sadness in my heart turned to hatred when her halfwit husband married again, only a few months after Gertrude's passing.

That woman never loved those children. Her distaste for them grew when she couldn't bear a child of her own. The herbs she begged from me didn't help. It was neither her fault nor mine. The relentless rain made more than just the ground infertile.

As soon as they were old enough, she worked those poor children from the moment she roused them awake, to when she sent them to bed before their father returned from his timber trade.

My dear friend would be heartbroken if she saw her gorgeous son and beautiful daughter now. Their eyes rimmed in red from all the tears, dull with no hope of a better tomorrow.

More and more, this despicable woman would look for reasons to send them to bed without their dinner. The meagre meal wouldn't stretch to all four of them, and she'd rather eat their share before their father returned. I tried to pass them bits of bread when they were gathering sodden wood along our shared boundary, but they were too frightened. Not even starvation could ease the fear their stepmother had instilled in them about the witch that watched them. Instead, I laid white pebbles in the brown dirt, to lead them to a small covered basket, filled with whatever I could scour from the diminishing markets. This they would eat, even when Gretel caught me watching from a distance, their fears finally soothed.

I kept them fed. For Gertrude. That woman and this wet would not take them.

One evening, as I limped along the forest edge to collect the empty basket and the white pebbles, I overheard a hushed conversation. Normally, I would creep away, not wanting to intrude on another's private discussions, but something made me stay. Something made me listen. I stilled behind a large tree and held my breath.

"We cannot keep them," the woman hissed into the darkness.

"I cannot do what you ask."

I glanced around the trunk and saw Hansel and Gretel's father bring his hands to his face. Their stepmother pressed against him, forgetting her curves were gone.

"Look at us. We are starving to death. Families all over are doing the same thing. Sending their children away to give everyone a chance to outlast this weather. There is no use for either of them here. We cannot grow vegetables in this rain. Our last cow died ten days ago. There wasn't even any meat on its bones. If you take them beyond the forest, to the next village, they will stand a chance and so will we. Hansel will find work and he will care for Gretel." She spoke of them with a warmth I had never witnessed.

"They are my children," he whimpered.

"Then do what is best. For all of us."

It was a lie. The children would not survive. I only hoped their father would see their stepmother for who she was and be the man that Gertrude had loved.

The following morning, Hansel puffed out his chest with pride, carrying his father's heavy axe past my fence. Gretel skipped ahead, her whole body was alive with the glee of spending the day with her father. I smiled. They were helping him with his tasks today. They hadn't done that in quite some time. He hadn't followed his wife's commands. Hopefully, her terrible words were just symptoms of the strain of looking after two little ones in these awful times. Not even she could be that cruel.

As they continued far down the path, their stepmother walked to their gate and watched them leave. The lines around my eyes were numerous, but my sight was that of a woman many years younger, and I saw her expression. Dread filled my bones as a wicked smile spread across those sharp cheekbones.

I hobbled to the window overlooking the path, but they had already disappeared into the deep woods. I was too late. My wretched body would never catch up to them. I crumpled into my chair, what a fool I had been.

Something came over me as I sat there in despair. A childhood memory with my grandmother. I muttered her incantations under my breath, wishing for the little ones to return. The words felt unfamiliar in my mouth and sounded foreign to my ears, but all day I remained by that window and willed the spell to work.

By dusk, I saw a large figure appear. My heart held still. Another formed beside it, smaller than the first. But only two. As they got closer, I sighed in relief to see Gretel as well – her father was carrying her on his back. With her bright blue eyes, she looked the splitting image of her mother as they walked along my fence line. It was her smile.

It worked; the spell had changed his mind. I had brought them home. And yet, I cursed myself. How stupid of me to sit by and take *any* risk with Gertrude's children. What if their father *had* done their stepmother's bidding? I would have failed my friend.

That evening, I scurried as fast as my ragged body would allow, across the tree roots that escaped the sodden ground, until I was near the window to their bedroom. I needed to see them, to make sure they were truly safe. I peered through the gap in the flimsy drape, candlelight casting shadows over their sleeping frames. Hansel's mouth was gaping open. I placed two ginger cookies on the inside ledge with one white stone – for the morning.

As I left, I heard their stepmother.

"You were supposed to leave them there," she shouted angrily.

"I couldn't do it. I just couldn't." Their father sobbed.

"We are all going to starve. Is that what you want? For me to starve to death."

He muttered something incomprehensible.

"I'll take care of it." Her whispered words were laced with poison. "Tomorrow." I wondered if he even heard her through his blubbering.

As I staggered back to my cottage, the pain of walking shot up my weary legs, and I recalled what I'd overheard in the markets. Mothers were sparing their children from starvation. Holding pillows over their faces as they slept. Drowning them in rivers. Hunger was a terrible disease. By the time I reached the wooden door of my home, I knew Gertrude's children were in mortal danger. Only I could save them from being killed in cold blood.

I found meine Otto's wooden chest covered in dust. I would need his maps. He was an explorer and had travelled much further than I ever had, or any woman in my family. He took pride in his maps, detailing them with such precision. They were decades old now, but the roads would still be the same. They would lead us far away from this danger.

All night I baked and wrapped and gathered what I thought we would need. It all had to fit into Otto's old rucksack and a potato bag that had laid empty in my kitchen for many years.

As the clouds emptied their load, their father left for the day. A little while later, I stood by the edge of the forest once more, gazing at the drenched landscape, holding my breath. What if she intended to kill them before they woke? Smoke from their chimney became thicker and I hoped it was Hansel stoking the flames. She wouldn't dirty her hands with the fire. Finally, once the rain stopped, two small figures emerged to tend to their daily chores. They trod around their house, through Gertrude's once beautiful flower garden, being careful of the mud pulling at their boots.

A tiny ray of sunshine poked through the clouds and fell perfectly. Gretel was the first to spot the glimmering stone. She pointed excitedly and Hansel found the second. They followed the small white pebbles until they found me, hunched under Otto's large and heavy black travel cape.

Gretel ducked behind Hansel, his narrow frame standing resolute to protect his sister.

"Please don't be afraid," I said. "I knew your mother."

At the mention of her mother, Gretel peered around.

"Before you were born." I kept her gaze, then looked at Hansel. "You were too little to remember, but your mother would visit me every evening with you, first tied to her chest, then trotting beside her as your sister grew in her belly."

Tears pooled on his eyelids.

"Thank you for the sweet biscuits." Gretel's voice was her mother's. "The ginger ones are my favourite."

I smiled at her kindness despite all the horribleness she witnessed each day. "You must come with me. It is not safe for you to stay here."

"Come with you? Where?" Hansel was alert but his tone respectful.

"I'm sorry, my little ones, but I fear your stepmother plans to kill you before nightfall. There is not enough food for all four of you and she won't sacrifice herself for you."

"My father wouldn't allow it." Hansel's jaw was set firm, the previous day's happiness still fresh in his mind.

"Your father is not the man who married your mother. He does the bidding of your stepmother. He took you out to the woods yesterday with instructions from her to leave you there. To abandon you."

"No, my father would never do that." Hansel raised his voice.

I glanced in the direction of their cottage, fearing the noise would draw her out.

The door remained closed.

"It's true, Hansel." Gretel's softness broke through her brother's anger. "I heard them speaking of it last night. I thought it was a nightmare. But it's true." Tears trickled down her hollowed cheeks as she understood her father's betrayal.

Hansel took her hand and looked at her for a minute before turning back to me. "When?" He asked.

"We need to leave right now." I showed him the two sacks bursting at the seams.

"Where?"

"Until the edges of the maps. Somewhere safe. Somewhere beyond your father's searches. I know he loves you and he will try to find you, I'm sure of it. But if he did, he would think nothing of bringing you back – to her. He does not see your stepmother the way she is, and her threat to be rid of you would only have grown stronger."

He let go of Gretel's hand and stepped forward, lifting the heavier of the two sacks on his spindly shoulders. I slung the other over my crooked bones, the weight crunching my joints. I willed them not to let me down. For Gertrude's children. I looked back at the home where my dear grandmother had been born. It was only now I noticed how dilapidated it was. Crumbling like a cookie.

Gretel stooped down and picked up one of the mud-speckled pebbles, rubbing the brown muck from it with her thumb. She gazed it at for a moment, before tucking it in her dress pocket.

"You will no longer need to follow stones for morsels of food, I will make sure of it," I said.

A few years on, as I traded my herbs for food in the markets with Gretel, I heard two women passing on news of a faraway town. A town where a Zauberin lived. To survive the famine, she took to luring children from their homes with little white pebbles where she would plump them up with sweets and biscuits before boiling them alive to have for her dinner. *Monstrous*, they whispered. *Those poor parents, to lose their children that way.*

They barely noticed me eavesdropping, for I was no longer seen as a witch but as a caring grandmother, looking after her two orphaned grandchildren. Exactly as Gertrude would want.

ABOUT 'HEZZE: THE GINGERBREAD HAG'

In the original Brothers Grimm fairy tale 'Hansel and Gretel', the witch who lures the children with her edible house before attempting to eat Hansel, is first introduced as a "very, very old woman". While she holds no magic to truly classify herself as a witch, her age is evil incarnate. Everything that comes with aging, the inability to walk without the use of "crutches" or her poor vision, is enough for youth to fear. In 'Hezze: The Gingerbread Hag', I challenge this villain archetype of old age – something we still have in our society's quest for perpetual youth. It is a reimagining of the original story from the perspective of a neighbour, ostracised as a sorcerer because of her knowledge of medicinal herbs, age-old wisdom passed down through generations. Instead of wanting to exact revenge on the world for her loneliness and decaying body, she holds her memories of kindness as debts she hopes she can repay. As a terrible famine plagues medieval Europe (rumoured to be where the idea for 'Hansel and Gretel' was born), Hezze opts to save her friend's children from a fate too many others faced. An opposite reaction to the youthful and once-beautiful stepmother.

ABOUT AVI VINCE

Avi Vince is an aspiring author working on her first novel. She has developed her craft attending various workshops at the Australian Writers' Centre and Faber Academy. She used to work as the Managing Editor of *Mamamia*, Australia's largest independent women's media group, and is now a freelance writer covering a broad range of topics.

ACKNOWLEDGEMENTS

―――――⌒〜⌒―――――

ZENA SHAPTER

Thank you to all the wonderful writers who collaborated and contributed to this extravaganza of creativity. Not only did every writer conjure their own unique stories, delving deep into the archetypes of their voice, but they spent many patient hours editing with me, restructuring, rewriting, and polishing until their stories shone. They also read and critiqued each other's work and proofread final versions, hunting through manuscripts for typos and mistakes. Thanks also to Nick Slessor and Mijmark for proofreading stories, it's lovely that you offered to help out.

We must also thank the many storytellers of the past who conceived such stories that established the archetypal villain types we have explored in this anthology, giving us our inspiration. Some stories and the archetypes they create can transverse time and place, giving insight into the human experience, and creating storytelling connections between writers. It's an honour to be a part of that conversation.

Finally, I'm sure everyone would like to thank their friends and families for their support, as I would like to thank mine – your support and acceptance are the backbone to everything I do. You know how I love stories.

Zena Shapter
Editor-in-Chief

Also by the
NORTHERN BEACHES WRITERS' GROUP

northernbeacheswritersgroup.com